Web of Conspiracy

Book Two

Patriots and Traitors

By

Herbert Grosshans

Published by
Melange Books, LLC
White Bear Lake, MN 55110
www.melange-books.com

Web of Conspiracy, Book 2, Patriots and Traitors,
Herbert Grosshans, Copyright © 2011

ISBN: 978-1-61235-025-7

Credits

Copy Edit: Tom Dahedl
Copy Editor: Nancy Schumacher
Format Editor: Mae Powers
Cover Artist: A. Bratt

About the Author

Herbert lives near Winnipeg, Canada. He spends his free time spinning tales about imaginary worlds and the strange creatures inhabiting them. His first published story `The Anniversary Gift' appeared in `Sweet Revenge' published by Midnight Showcase. Even though he writes in other genres, his love is Science Fiction. He enjoys building alien worlds and societies. Most of his stories contain an element of Erotica. All of his books are available from Melange Books.

Website: http://www.hegro.shawwebspace.ca
Blog: http://hegro.blogspot.comEmail: hegro@shaw.ca

Web of Conspiracy

Book Two, Patriots and Traitors

By Herbert Grosshans

Jeff Chartrand and his team are sent to Iraq on a covert mission. They discover a threat that could escalate the war in the Middle East. His investigation leads him to one of the men responsible for his brother's murder. Jeff is torn between three women.

Works also by and including Herbert Grosshans:
Stars In Chains 1, Slave
Stars In Chains 2: Liberator
Stardogs 1 & 2
The Xandra Triology
Cliffs of Time
Orion the Hunt
Beyond the Stars Digest
Orion: Symbiont of Passion
Men of Eros
Web of Conspiracy, Book 1, Death of a Hero

Prologue

When Detective Jeff Chartrand and his partner Maxine Montana are sent to investigate a shooting, he finds his brother Michael, his sister-in-law Samantha, and his nephew Joseph murdered. Victims of a drug deal gone wrong, according to Detective Sheppard, but Jeff does not believe it. He is taken off the case for personal reasons. When they find evidence that Michael might have had connections to Joseph Galliano, a known mobster, Jeff decides to look up Galliano. According to Galliano, Michael owes him five thousand dollars, money he lost gambling. Galliano wants his money, but Jeff tells him he has to wait for it.

Michael Chartrand was a decorated war hero. He served in Iraq, where he was a member of a unit they called the *Ten Commandos*. When Jeff tries to contact one of Michael's war buddies, he finds that he and his wife have been shot to death in their apartment. Another one, Dennis Kim, lies in a Fresno hospital, in a coma, after someone beat him up in an apparent botched robbery. Jeff drives to Fresno and meets Connie Wu, Kim's roommate. She shows him pictures of the soldiers who were the *Ten Commandos.*

One of men in the pictures, Ronald Larkin, the CO of the unit, is now running for Senator, but his ultimate goal is to become President of the United States.

Connie believes that the two murders and the attack on her friend Dennis are connected. She suspects that Ronald Larkin's life might be in danger. Jeff and Connie feel an attraction for each other and before Jeff drives home, he and Connie make love. She is the first woman he has been intimate with since his wife's death.

Among Michael's belongings Jeff finds a key to a safety deposit box, part of a journal, and an envelope with some photos of a dark haired girl holding a baby. He also discovers that Michael sent two hundred dollars every month to Iraq through the local mosque.

Jeff and Montana go to one of Larkin's campaigns and try to tell him that he might be next on the list, but Larkin is not worried. "I have a good bodyguard in John Parker. He keeps me safe." John Parker is one of the *Ten Commandos*. Larkin shows an interest in Michael's journal and he wants to know if there are any pictures or other stuff from Iraq.

When Jeff and Montana drive home, she tells him she wants him to make love to her. He has never thought of her as a woman before, just his partner, but suddenly he finds her quite attractive and he takes her home to his apartment. She spends the night with him.

A few days later, when Jeff and Montana come home from a dinner, a man by the name of Ethan Grey tries to shoot him and Jeff kills him in self-defense. Ethan Grey is another former member of the *Ten Commandos*. He has with him an attaché case with pictures of Jeff and the other members of the unit. It seems, Ethan Grey was the assassin, but Jeff is not convinced.

When Jeff arrives at the precinct after the shootout, he is interviewed by two agents from Homeland Security. Agent Dave MacKay and Agent Manning. They are accusing him of having ties to the Muslim community and to Al Queda. They show him a printout of a bank account with his and Michael's name on it. There are over hundred thousand dollars on the account. Jeff has no idea that account existed, but the agents don't believe him. Dave MacKay is the twin brother of John MacKay, who was also a member of the *Ten Commandos*. He apparently died by friendly fire in Iraq, just like Darrin Montana, Maxine's brother.

Internal Affairs suspends Jeff. He tells Maxine (Montana) about his time in the army, tells her that he was a member of Grey Ops, a special unit in Army Intelligence, and that he is contemplating going back to his old unit.

Jeff finds an SD card in a safety box belonging to his brother. On it are disturbing images...pictures of American soldiers helping Iraqis unloading boxes from US Military vehicles. There is even a small video depicting the rape of an Iraqi girl and her murder by American soldiers.

While visiting his sister, Jeff meets Werner Reinhart, a German. Reinhart is an old friend of Jeff's brother-in-law. Jeff has misgivings about the jovial German, who comes across like a friendly, charming gentleman. It turns out that Reinhart is a mercenary and he seems to remember Michael from Iraq.

Jeff drives back to Fresno to talk to a Detective Smith, who has shown an interest in Jeff's problem. He finds out that Dennis Kim has been shot to death in his hospital bed. He spends the night with Connie. He promises her to be back for the funeral.

After arriving home, he finds a message on his answering machine asking him to meet with Colonel Cowley, his former commander. Cowley asks Jeff to join the unit again. Only then will he be able to help him with his search for his brother's murderer.

That same day, he meets a woman, who introduces herself as Kalila Ahmed. She tells him she is the sister of the girl in the photos Jeff found among Michael's possessions. The little baby is Michael's son. His name is Omar. She also tells him her sister has been stoned to death by the people in her village, because she committed an unforgivable sin. Omar is now in an orphanage.

Jeff also meets two Iraqi men, who want back the twenty thousand dollars they deposited in Michael's account before he was murdered. He tells them he knows nothing about the money. The men warn him that things might get ugly if they don't get their money back.

In the meantime, Galliano has been phoning Jeff's sister demanding the five thousand dollars, except now he wants thirty thousand. Jeff pays him another visit. During the confrontation, he kills Galliano and his body guard Tony Moretti. He is arrested for the murder and taken into custody. One of the arresting officers is Maxine Montana.

Elias Morgan, an attorney, gets Jeff out of jail. Morgan reveals that he has been with Grey Ops since its conception and he knows everything about Jeff. Jeff is hiding out in a safe house owned by the Military.

A group that calls itself *The Needle of Allah* kidnaps Omar, Michael's son. Colonel Cowley sends Jeff and his new team to Iraq to rescue the little boy. Accompanying him are Cowley's son Rob Masters and Kalila, the Iraqi woman who claimed to be Omar's aunt. She works for Iraqi Intelligence and came to America to stop the selling of arms to insurgents.

Chapter One

It was thirty-seven degrees centigrade when the seven men and one woman climbed out of the plane. The heat hit them with full force, and before they had taken half a dozen steps, Jeff Chartrand could smell the dust in the dry air. He was tired after the long flight and wanted to take a bath and sleep for the next few days, but he knew both things would be something denied to him.

Colonel Settler turned out to be a short, heavyset man with a bushy mustache. If it weren't for the US army uniform, he could have been mistaken for an Iraqi.

He and two dust-covered soldiers carrying automatic weapons met the eight people and, without much ado, they hustled them toward a metal building, which seemed to serve as headquarters.

Before they entered the building, Jeff looked back to see the plane being unloaded by a group of soldiers. He didn't envy them. Working in this murderous heat was surely no easy task.

The Colonel took them into a small room. The air was hot and sticky inside the building. A single bulb hung from the ceiling, probably powered by a generator. Obviously, there was no power left for air-conditioning.

Colonel Settler must have detected Jeff's discomfort and chuckled. "This is not the Ritz, as you may have noticed. I'd offer you something cold to quench your thirst, but the water is not fit to drink and our fridge broke down."

He took a seat behind a metal desk and pulled out a thick envelope. Handing it to Jeff, he said, "Here are your orders, Lieutenant Chartrand, and the latest information we received from our spies. How correct it is, we don't know. It also contains a map of Baghdad and the surrounding region, pinpointing checkpoints and problem areas."

He chuckled. "Of course, all of Iraq is a problem area. There are no safe havens anywhere. Once you leave the base, you're on your own. If things get hairy, don't expect any help from us. Officially, you are not here."

He looked at Kalila. "Lieutenant Ahmed, this is your country and we have no jurisdiction over you outside this base and we cannot offer you any protection. I understand you are expecting to be contacted by your superiors?"

She nodded. "Actually, I will have to contact them. They do not know I am here."

"I know I can't command you to follow my request, but I would suggest you do not reveal your real reason for coming back right now. You cannot trust anyone, not even your own people. Once this mission is over, you can do whatever you want, but I don't want you to put our men in danger." Colonel Settler twirled his mustache. "I understand you have a personal stake in this?"

"Yes, I do. The kidnapped boy is my sister's son. I have more than just a passing interest in the success of this mission."

The Colonel looked her over. "I guess I don't have to tell you once you exchange your US army uniform for your local dress, you'd be advised to cover your face, for you own safety. Things are getting worse every day."

She smiled. "I am well aware of that, Colonel Settler, but thank you for your concern."

"We're about thirty minutes from the outskirts of Baghdad. You'll be taken to one of our bases in downtown Baghdad. It used to be a hotel, but not too many visitors come to Baghdad anymore." He chuckled over his own joke. "The rooms there are limited, so I've put you and Lieutenant Ahmed together into one room. As far as anyone is concerned, you two are married." He smiled thinly. "I hope you don't mind. As I understand you two have been living together already in the States."

"We have, but not as husband and wife," Kalila said. "And just to make things clear, Lieutenant Chartrand and I are not involved in any relationship."

"Nothing like that was suggested," Settler said.

"I have no problem with sharing a room with Lieutenant Ahmed,"

Jeff said. "As long as we have separate beds." His eyes flicked to Kalila, but she didn't say anything.

Colonel Settler rubbed his hands. "Well, then we won't have a problem. You'll be traveling in an armored vehicle and you'll be relatively safe but..." His face looked grim. "Nothing is guaranteed in this country. Never let down your guard. Suicide bombers can pop up anywhere. Now they're even using women. These people have no regard for human life." He gave Kalila an apologetic look. "Sorry, but that's the impression I have. Many of us have. Why else would people blow themselves and others up like that? What kind of person would kill innocent school children?"

"I cannot tell you that, Colonel. Perhaps people who do not know where to turn because they are so frustrated and have nothing to lose. People who want to make a difference," Kalila said. If she felt annoyed or angry about the Colonel's remark, her voice and face didn't betray her feelings.

"If these bombings and attacks on innocent people would stop, maybe we would leave your country and go home to our families, but it seems you can't decide what government should rule in your country." He shrugged. "Not that it really makes a difference. Whatever faction finally wins will make live miserable for the others of different religions. The bloodshed will continue."

"If you feel that way, Colonel Settler, why do you not pack up and leave now?" Kalila asked, her voice still calm, but Jeff felt the ice in the air.

The Colonel stared at her for a moment, his eyes glazed over, and then he smiled. "Forgive me if I insulted you, Miss Ahmed. I mean that. I'm just venting. This damn heat is getting to me. I care very much what happens to your people, otherwise I wouldn't be here." He paused. "I guess you should be going. I'll have you escorted to your transportation."

He rose and came around the desk. Holding out a hand to Jeff, he said, "Good luck, Lieutenant Chartrand. I hope your mission is successful and you all come back alive. This war is different from the one we fought in 1991. Be careful."

Jeff was surprised that the Colonel mentioned the Gulf War. Obviously, he had been briefed about Jeff in detail.

He shook the offered hand. "Thank you, Colonel." Then he saluted, turned to join the others who were already filing out of the door and following the two armed soldiers.

It had been hot inside the building, but when they stepped outside, the hot air washed over them like a blast from a furnace. Jeff was already drenched down to his underwear and when he climbed into the armored truck, he leaned back into his seat, wishing he had something cold to drink and an air-conditioned vehicle.

Kalila took the seat beside him. The heat didn't seem to affect her as much as it did him, because she didn't look flushed. His face felt hot and prickly as if he had spent hours trudging under the burning sun.

Looking out of the window, he could see soldiers walking around in their camouflage outfits, their bodies loaded down with heavy weapons and ammunition. He remembered his time in Kuwait, in the desert, with temperatures just as stifling, but somehow he didn't remember suffering this much.

He turned around to check on Rob and the other men. They didn't look stressed. At least they gave that impression.

I guess this war is for young men, not for old guys in their forties.

After their gear had been stowed in the back of the vehicle, they finally got underway. He noticed another vehicle in front of him and another one in the rear. The dust rose up all around them as they traveled the bumpy road, heading east, toward Baghdad.

Thirty minutes to the outskirts of Baghdad the Colonel had told them. That meant at least an hour until they would reach their destination, possibly even longer. And it seemed to be getting hotter. If that was at all possible.

Damn you, Michael! I'm here only because of you and that child you had to father. Why couldn't you keep that prick of yours in your pants? Why, brother, why?

He felt angry and frustrated. Not a good thing. He needed to keep his cool.

He grinned at the pun.

He needed to keep his cool. Right.

A cold beer would be much appreciated right now, and a hot naked woman in an air-conditioned bedroom would not be a bad thing, either.

Sighing, he closed his eyes and tried to pretend he was sitting in a bus heading for a resort in one of the tropical islands, but it proved impossible, tired as he was and drenched in his own perspiration.

"How do you like my country this far?"

Jeff opened his eyes when he heard Kalila's voice. He had some trouble focusing for a moment; his tired body seemed to have gone into hibernation. He realized he had dozed off, after all. Straightening his body, he gave her a small grin. "Are you sure we haven't died and ended up in hell?" he joked.

She didn't smile. "No such luck. Do you know that, according to legends, the Garden of Eden is supposed to have been somewhere here in Iraq?"

Jeff chuckled. "No wonder Adam and Eve left. I would have."

"They did not leave. They were evicted." She smiled. "Did you forget?"

"I'm not that up anymore on religious legends. They are not on my mind these days. I've been disillusioned by all this hatred and destruction happening on this great planet that was supposed to have been created by a loving God. I see no love anywhere. We've been abandoned."

She touched his hand again, fleetingly, as if afraid he might push it away. He wouldn't have. "I am a Muslim and I do not hate you because of your belief. Not every Muslim hates Christians or anyone else who worships differently, no matter what your media is telling you. We want peace just like every citizen of this *Great Planet*, as you put it. There is enough room for everyone. Paradise can be created again, but we must all do our bit to make it happen."

"You said every citizen wants peace. I wish it were so. There are plenty of crazy fanatics out there who will do anything to create havoc in the name of religion. Here in your country. That is the reason we are here, Kalila," he said bitterly. "I'm trying my best to bring peace. I was a cop, remember?"

"I know, but you are wrong if you want to blame everything on religion. I do not believe this war has anything to do with religion. It is all about who controls the oil in the Middle East. The Gulf War was the beginning of this war."

"That is correct. Do you also know the reason?" Jeff asked. "I'll tell you. Because Saddam Hussein invaded Kuwait. He wanted to increase Iraq's share of world oil reserves."

"Iraq invaded Kuwait because they stole oil from Iraq by drilling into our oilfields," Kalila countered. She smiled again. "You just admitted this war is not over religion but over politics. Like most wars on our planet. Religion is just an excuse for our leaders. It is a powerful motivator. It just so happens the Middle East is populated by Muslims. That makes us the enemy. Would it have been inhabited by Hindus or Buddhists they would have been the enemy?"

"You are forgetting something. The men who attacked America on September 11, 2001 were Muslim extremists. Osama Bin Laden is a Muslim."

"That is true. I cannot argue with that," Kalila agreed. "But Osama Bin Laden is not an Iraqi. He is a member of the Saudi Royal Family. Do not forget that."

Jeff chuckled. "I didn't know you were so interested in world affairs. It appears there is more behind your beautiful face than a man would assume."

"Now you are talking like most men again. Women are not stupid. Some of us are smarter than men. Maybe this world should be run by women. I bet there would be fewer wars."

"You'd make a good spokeswoman for Women's Lib." He studied her face, as she looked at him, her eyes dark and warm, almost affectionate, even after his comment. "I mean that as a compliment, not a derogative remark," he said, feeling like taking her into his arms. She looked so vulnerable at this moment, and so passionate, but he knew, that passion was not for him. She felt strongly about the things she told him.

It made her only more attractive to him.

* * * *

Traveling through Baghdad was slow and tedious. The people in the streets looked anxious and scared. Most women were veiled. Policemen, their rifles in plain sight, traveled in groups, their parked cars not as new and shiny as the ones back in the States. Buildings that had once been beautiful now were only ugly, bombed-out husks, skeletons of former beautiful architecture.

The hotel still looked like a hotel from the outside, but when the group entered the lobby, it became obvious this was not a place for tourists. Not anymore.

A couple of armed soldiers met them and took them up to the third floor. As the Colonel had told them, Jeff shared a room with Kalila.

"This must be the honeymoon suite," Jeff joked, taking in the spacious living room and then giving Kalila a leering stare.

She laughed. "Typical male. You look like you are dying from the heat, but you are still thinking about sex." Then she favored him with a coquette smile. "If we were really married, I might just let you have your way but..."she shrugged, "...we are not. If you do not mind, I am going to take a quick bath."

Jeff moved his pack into one of the bedrooms. There was a double bed, but he doubted that it would be used by two people. Not this time. The furnishings in the suite looked western, clearly a sign that it was designed for foreign visitors, possibly dignitaries from Western or European countries.

He could hardly wait for Kalila to finish taking her bath. Right now he wanted nothing more than wash the grime from his body. Rummaging around in his pack, he found a change of clothing; a pair of thin pants, a short-sleeved shirt, and new underwear. Then he lay on his bed, watching the door to the bathroom.

When Kalila finally emerged, she had a towel wrapped around herself. He noticed the small bundle of clothing in her hand. "I am finished," she called, sticking her head into his room.

Grabbing his own clothing, he went into the vacated bathroom, expecting to find some kind of exotic-looking tub, but he was surprised to see a regular tub. It didn't even have a shower.

The next surprise was the water pressure, which was next to nothing, and the water flowing out the tab was warm. However, it was heaven to be able to wash his body and to change into dry clothing.

When he walked out of the bathroom, he found Kalila in the living room, wearing black pants and a white blouse. He whistled softly when he saw her. "Are you trying to seduce me?" he asked.

"No, I am not." She laughed. "Do you like it?"

"How can I not? You look smashing in that outfit."

"I am glad you think so. I bought it in America." She sighed a little. "Unfortunately, I will never be able to wear this in public, only in my own home."

Jeff took a seat across from her. Made out of wood, the chair looked a bit out of place, but it felt comfortable. "If you hate it so much here, why don't you move away, to another country? Like America?"

"How could I ever move away? This is my homeland. I was born here. There is nothing wrong with my country except what has been done to it. By my own people and by foreigners. Mainly by Americans."

A knock on the door announced a visitor. Jeff went to open it and found Rob standing in the hallway. He handed Jeff a couple of boxes. Jeff recognized them for what they where.

Army rations.

Rob grinned, seeing Jeff's enthusiastic expression. "I've ordered a gourmet meal for you and Miss Ahmed. Enjoy."

"Well, thank you Rob. You shouldn't have. Where is the wine?"

Rob shrugged. "We're temporarily out," he said, playing along, "but I hope the juice will be a satisfactory substitute."

"I guess it will do." Jeff became serious. "I want everyone to get a good night's rest. We will meet in the morning."

Rob saluted. "Yes, sir, Lieutenant. I will tell the men." He saluted again. Jeff returned the salute.

As a civilian, he had scoffed at the rigid military way he had left behind, but it was becoming easier every day to fall back into that life. He'd better. After all, he was the leader of the team and the highest-ranking officer.

When the door closed behind Rob, he suddenly remembered something.

Putting the two small packages on the small table, he said, "You never told me that you are a lieutenant in the Iraqi army."

Kalila looked up from some papers she'd been studying. "There was no need to tell you. For your information, I am not in the army. I work for Iraqi Intelligence."

"What's the difference?" Jeff said. "You still work for the government."

"No, I am not. We take no political sides."

Jeff chuckled, as if amused by her comment. "When Saddam was in power, didn't you work for him then? Was the Iraqi Intelligence Service not just another arm of Saddam Hussein's spy net?"

"Not the branch I am working for. We are totally independent." She smiled. "I am sure you have an agency like that in America, right?

Maybe even more than one?"

Jeff shrugged, remembering his own missions. Not all of them had been sanctioned by his government. He wasn't even sure about the one he was on right now.

Had Colonel Cowley followed orders from somebody higher up or was this on his own shoulders? Kalila told him she had done a little bit of arm-twisting with the Colonel. How much of that had actually been necessary? Jeff wondered about the Colonel's hidden agenda. There always was one. Somebody had to approve the expenditures for this mission. For any mission.

Somebody was keeping books.

"I guess we have," he said slowly.

They ate in silence. When they were finished, Jeff threw the empty boxes into a trashcan.

As the evening progressed, the lights suddenly went out.

"What happened now?" Jeff asked with a sharp voice.

"No need to get alarmed," Kalila said soothingly. "This happens all the time. I guess this part of the city, or maybe just this building, has used up its allotted amount of power."

"Wonderful!" Jeff cursed. "I guess this means the end of our air-conditioning? Just when we need it most! How far does the temperature drop down at night?"

"It may go down to thirty degrees. If we are lucky" Kalila chuckled. "You just have to sleep naked. I do."

He couldn't see her in the dark, but he heard her moving on the couch. The picture of her lying naked on her bed formed in his mind's eye. It didn't help.

"You know, if this were in the United States I'd know how to spend the dark night. It wouldn't be so bad. In fact, a blackout always adds to the excitement," he said, making his voice low and seductive sounding. "Just me and a beautiful young woman, eager and willing to please me. Both of us naked. Aren't Iraqi women expected to please their men?"

Kalila chuckled in the dark. "They are, but you are not my man, so forget it!"

Jeff sighed. "I'm only fantasizing, that's all. I realize there is a huge difference between my world and yours. Too bad."

She stayed silent for a while, and then she suddenly said, "Were you and your former partner lovers?"

Her blunt question took him by surprise. How should he answer? Maxine and he had made love only once. Sure, they would have done it again, had planned to do it again. It never happened because circumstances did not permit it to happen. Did that make them lovers?

"No," he answered. "We were not lovers, but we could have been. Under different circumstances." This was not quite the truth, either. Had it not been for the traumatic experience with Michael's murder and the events that followed it, his relationship with Maxine probably would never have moved past the professional level.

"She is an attractive woman." Kalila said.

"How do you know that?"

Kalila's disembodied voice floated across the room. "I told you before I make it a point to familiarize myself with the people I work with. That also includes the people they are associating with." She chuckled softly. "It is part of my training."

"You still have the advantage over me," Jeff said. "You seem to know everything about me, while I know next to nothing about you, aside from the things you told me."

"Maybe that will change some day, who knows," she said enigmatically.

He heard her get up and walk around, her bare feet making tiny sucking sounds on the hard floor. His eyes had adjusted to the darkness and it didn't seem so complete anymore. He could see her faint shadow against the outline of the window.

Cautiously, her hands in front of her, she walked over to a closet and opened it. Then, suddenly, a light flared up and he saw the candle in her hand.

"Not enough to read by," she said, a little smile playing around her lips, while the weak light from the flickering flame played hide and seek with the darkness obscuring her features.

She put the candle on the table. "I am going to bed, anyway," she announced. Before she disappeared into her bedroom, she said over her shoulder, "Good night, I hope you sleep well."

Chapter Two

Despite her well-wishes, he didn't sleep well. The temperature rose rapidly, and when he opened the window the air coming in from the outside was hot and dusty.

"How can people survive in this damn country?" he cursed. "They should concentrate their efforts on making it hospitable for themselves, instead of planning bombings and suicides."

Kalila was already up and dressed when he rose from his bed, tired and feeling miserable. "Sleep well?" she asked with a smile. When she saw his grumpy face, she shook her head. "You Americans, you have grown soft with all of your amenities and comfortable homes and vehicles."

"Perhaps we have," Jeff growled, "but we enjoy life. Most of the time anyway, until somebody, who is jealous of our lifestyle and thinks we should change it, tries to disrupt our lives." He ran his hand across his beard. "Damn thing is starting to itch. I hope there is water."

"There is and the power is back on. Or have you not noticed?"

Only now, he realized the light in the hallway was on. He also began to feel the cooler temperature. "At least some good news," he grumbled. "If Rob brings us our breakfast, I believe I might just survive this day."

He looked at her more closely, noticing her mode of dress. "Going somewhere?"

She nodded and smoothed out the dark fabric that covered her from head to ankle. A black shawl framed her face. "I am afraid you will have to eat breakfast alone. I will be going out to meet with my people. Maybe I can gather some more information."

"Be careful," he warned her, feeling suddenly protective and apprehensive about her decision. "I thought we were in this together?"

"We are, but there are some things I need to do by myself." She favored him with a friendly smile. "Do not worry, I am a big girl and I can take care of myself. Remember, this is my home country."

"Isn't a woman supposed to be accompanied by a man when she goes out in public?" he asked, still concerned.

"I will be picked up be someone. I will not be alone."

Before he could say much more, she walked out the door.

He didn't like her wandering around Baghdad by herself but, as she pointed out, this was her country. She knew what to expect better than he did, and he didn't doubt she could defend herself it attacked. However, there was not much defense against some crazy fanatic blowing himself to smithereens and her with it, if she stood close enough.

He washed his face and combed his hair and beard, feeling much better. As if on cue, Rob knocked against the door, and when Jeff unlocked and opened it, Rob saluted smartly. "Good morning, sir. Breakfast."

"Have you eaten?" Jeff asked.

"No, sir, but the men and I are going to do so as soon as I return to our room."

"Do you mind if I join you? Miss Ahmed decided to go exploring."

"We'd be honored, sir." Rob turned to leave. "Just follow me."

Jeff was surprised when he entered the suite Rob and the others occupied. The door to one of the bedrooms stood open, and when he took a closer look, he saw computer screens and other electronic equipment.

Rob saw him looking. "We've set up some cots in the other bedroom," he said. "We're using this one as our command post. Do you want to inspect it?"

Jeff nodded and walked into the room. "Where does all this stuff come from?" he asked, looking at the different screens.

"We brought it with us," Rob said.

"What's it for?"

"Surveillance, sir. We'll be able to track your movements over the satellite. Just some additional insurance, that's all."

"What about when the power gets shut off?"

"No problem. We have our own backup."

Jeff shook his head. "You know, I'm not up on this modern electronic stuff. I can barely work my computer. I guess I'm an old dinosaur."

Rob grinned. "This is my specialty, sir. I've designed some of this stuff myself." He pointed to one of the screens. It showed a highlighted object moving slowly along a dark strip, which he recognized as a street as seen from an airplane or helicopter.

"The green dot inside that object is Miss Ahmed. She's inside a car that picked her up a few minutes ago."

"What the hell!" Jeff cursed. "How did you manage that?"

"Manage what, sir?"

"Plant a bug on her."

"I put it inside her purse, back in the States." Rob gave him an innocent little boy's grin. "I like to plan ahead."

"Where did you plant mine? I'm not carrying a purse." Jeff eyed the young man suspiciously.

"You don't have one, sir. Not yet."

"Why not me? Why Miss Ahmed?"

"You're one of us. She's a foreigner. A spy." He lifted his shoulders. "I don't trust her. Neither should you."

Jeff chuckled grimly. "She's the aunt of that little boy. Why would she betray us?"

"She says she is the aunt. We don't know that. We have only her word." He looked at Jeff, his face suddenly changed from a sixteen years old boy to that of a hundred year old wise man. "Some people live by the motto *Love everyone, trust few, harm no one.* I love few, trust none, harm the ones who mean to do me harm."

"You're a cynical young man," Jeff said. "You need help."

Rob smiled. "My father, the Colonel, taught me that philosophy. He's lived by it, and he seems to do all right."

"Colonel Cowley is a man I greatly admire, but he's not only a soldier, he's also a politician." Jeff sighed, watching the moving dot on the screen. "I think I'm getting too soft for this kind of work. Maybe that's why I left it behind."

"You became a cop. Not exactly a soft, peaceful job," Rob commented.

"That's correct, but at least I don't have to spy on the people I work with. I trust them. Some of them with my life." He thought of Maxine, wondering if his trust in her had been misplaced. She seemed to have abandoned him when he needed her.

It's easy to love and trust someone when everything goes well. What if disaster strikes? What if things turn upside down and the rest of the world wants your head? Shouldn't your friends stick with you?

He shrugged mentally. *I guess when the chips are down, you'll find out who your true friends really are.* Unfortunately, he didn't seem to have any left. Except maybe Connie. The smell of freshly brewed coffee tore him out of his dark thoughts.

"How about a cup of coffee, Lieutenant?" Rob asked.

"Don't mind if I do," Jeff said, giving the screen one last look, doubts creeping into his mind. Should he trust Kalila? She was, after all, a foreigner. An Iraqi. Her country occupied by another country…his country.

They had not exactly formed a deep friendship, even though they had spent time together in close proximity. Almost like an old married couple. No sex, just friends who are comfortable with each other.

No, Rob. You're wrong about her. I've looked into her eyes, and she into mine. I didn't see any treachery in those large brown eyes.

They joined the other five members of the team at the table in the living room. Jeff noticed this suite was identical to the one he shared with Kalila and, except for the large table the furnishings were the same.

The men nodded when he sat down, but they didn't salute. However, they made room for Rob, letting him sit on the only upholstered chair. Jeff realized suddenly who the real leader of the team actually was. He was the stranger among them, a relic from the past. This decade belonged to the younger generation, not his, but he was determined not to let on that he knew. "Good coffee," he commented.

"I smuggled it in from the States." Sergeant Abduk grinned. "I hope I don't get reprimanded for that, sir."

"I'll overlook it this time," Jeff said, smiling. "By the way, isn't anyone watching the screens?" He pointed a thumb in the direction of the bedroom.

"No need. I'm recording everything. We can check it later," Rob said.

"I've studied the envelope I received yesterday," Jeff said. "The location of the group calling itself *The Needle of Allah* is supposed to be near Al Kut, but Miss Ahmed is trying to see if she can get us more recent information." He didn't mention his irritation of the fact Kalila had gone out without consulting him. It wasn't their business. Neither was his concern for her.

"May I ask you a question, sir?"

"Go ahead, Specialist Harmon."

"Are you and Lieutenant Ahmed lovers?"

Jeff was not prepared for a personal question like that from a subordinate. Harmon gave him a questioning look. Jeff noticed that the others were also watching closely. At first, he wanted to give Harmon a sharp retort, but then he shrugged. "No, we're not. Why do you ask?"

"She is an Iraqi, an unknown factor. She works for Iraqi Intelligence and we have concerns about her. Even you, sir, with all due respect, pose a certain risk to the success of the mission. We are a team. We trust each other and we will not allow anyone or anything to compromise us. Should she pose a threat, we will eliminate her. I hope you understand that, sir."

His blue eyes were cold when he said that, and Jeff shuddered inside, believing every word Harmon said. He was transported back twenty years, to a time when he might have spoken the exact same words, and realized how far removed he was from that time. "You won't have to," he said softly. "If it should become necessary I will deal with her myself, but I appreciate your candor."

"Understood, sir." Harmon visibly relaxed, as did the others.

"Another cup of coffee, sir?" Rob asked politely.

"Sure, thank you," Jeff said, opening his package. "I think I'll start eating my breakfast."

* * * *

Jeff spent the day in his room, studying the map of Baghdad and the countryside surrounding the city. He concentrated mostly on the area south of Baghdad. That's where the insurgents presumably were holding Omar hostage. There had been no more news ever since that first broadcast, and Jeff was hoping time had not run out for the little boy.

Anger rose up in him, thinking about the mentality of men who would kidnap a three-year-old boy and use him as a bargaining tool, even threaten to kill him if their demands were not met. He asked himself the question he had been asking many times...what kind of people would commit such an unspeakable act? And all this in the name of religion and their god. As always, he didn't find an answer.

Kalila came back in the late afternoon.

"Have you found out anything?" he asked, trying hard not to look at her purse when she put it on the chair.

She nodded and took off her *Shaw*. "Our target is not in Al Kut but in Ash Shatrah, or near it," she told him. "However, we must move fast. They are getting impatient."

"We'll move tomorrow," Jeff said. "I'll let the men know." He looked at her, as she sat down on the chesterfield. "How did you come by that information?"

"I have informants." She smiled. "I believe you call them *snitches* in your country."

She pulled up the hem of her *abayah*, exposing her knees. "It is hot out there, even for me, and I'm not thrilled about wearing these long dark clothes. I am going to take a bath before the power goes out again."

He stared at her legs, admiring the shape of her calves. Then he looked into her hauntingly dark eyes. *She is so beautiful on the outside and her eyes seem to mirror the true beauty of her soul. I can't believe she would betray me.*

Tilting her head, she smiled at him. "Is anything wrong?" she asked, knowing with the intuitive powers of a woman that something was amiss.

He shook his head. "Your face looks flushed. I find you very attractive like this."

Laughing, she rose. "You are incorrigible. Are you that starved for a woman's attention?"

"Looking at you reminds me of how much I am," he told her.

When she was in the bathroom, he decided to visit the team and fill the men in on his plan. "I'm only taking Sergeant Abduk and Lieutenant Ahmed with me," he told them. "The rest of you will be on standby, monitoring our progress from here. Moving with the whole team through an area swarming with insurgents might draw too much attention. Besides, Sergeant Abduk and Miss Ahmed speak Arabic. I, at least, look like one. The rest I can fake."

Rob didn't like the plan. Neither did the others. "It is my decision. If things go wrong, you can move in. At the very least, you can revenge our deaths."

Chapter Three

As Kalila had informed them would happen, a car pulled up in front of the hotel at seven A.M. It looked old and battered, had obviously seen better days.

The driver came out to greet them with a friendly smile. He spoke first to Kalila, but then he turned to Jeff and said, "I am Zalmay Hamid. I speak American. I will take you to your destination in my humble car. I ask for nothing in return except you must pay for the petrol." He gave Jeff a toothless smile. "Petrol is scarce in Baghdad and very expensive. A thousand dinars for one liter. I am a poor man, I cannot afford that."

It seemed strange to hear him say that gasoline was in short supply in a country that was oil-rich, but Jeff knew it to be the truth. "If you take us where we want to go, I'll promise you more than just reimbursement for your expenditures," Jeff said. "You'll have enough money to feed your family for a long time."

Hamid grabbed Jeff's hand and kissed it. "You are most generous. Long live America."

While Jeff talked to the driver, he watched Rob walking around the car, bending down, as if examining it. He didn't miss when Rob's hand lingered underneath the frame by the passenger's side. Rob straightened out, apparently satisfied with his inspection. His eyes met Jeff's and he gave him a quick smile. "I think the car will get you around," he said as he came back.

"Of course it will," Hamid said. "I am taking good care of it. It may not look new, but it is sound. Do not worry." He looked expectantly at Jeff. "Are you ready to leave?"

"Yes, we are."

As the driver walked back to his car, Jeff said to Rob in a low voice, "Everything all right?"

Rob nodded. "We'll know where the car will be."

"How about me?" Jeff asked.

"You, too, sir." Rob smiled.

Rob and his team could track the car and its occupants via satellite. Unfortunately, they would not be able to communicate with the team. Even though each of them wore a tiny flesh colored device inside one ear, not easily detected by a casual observer, they could only communicate with each other. The range of those communicators was too short.

Kalila and Abduk took their places on the backseat, while Jeff joined the driver in the front. He shoved his pack filled with a few bottles of water and a box of crackers under his seat. They could go without food but not without water. The day was already beginning to heat up. It promised to be another scorcher in hell.

All three were dressed in local garb. Kalila wore her *abayah*, a black dress that covered her from her shoulders down to her feet. Jeff and Abduk wore a white *dishdashan*, a long sleeved one-piece dress. The traditional headpiece covered their heads. Underneath the long dress, they wore army pants, with plenty of pockets to hide ammunition and an automatic. Jeff also carried a wad of Iraqi dinars. Enough to pay for the gasoline and possibly some bribes.

No papers that could identify them as Americans.

Ash Shatra, their destination, was approximately one hundred seventy-five miles south of Baghdad. In the States, on a good highway, they could reach it in about three hours, depending how fast they traveled. Here, in this country with an infrastructure in need of repairs, it could take all day.

Hamid drove his car skillfully through the traffic, avoiding pedestrians, who walked in the middle of the street. A few times, they met farmers herding small flocks of sheep through congested streets littered with rubble and twisted pieces of metal. Besides cars, trucks, and military vehicles, including tanks, they encountered riders on camels, and even on horses. A number of farmers headed for the market places with their vegetables in carts pulled by a lonely donkey.

Jeff noticed that some men were dressed in western clothing, while many wore the traditional white *dishdashan*. Old men, their heads covered by red and white checkered headpieces, sat on the hard ground, leaning against bombed out concrete buildings, their bearded, lined faces somber, their eyes watchful and resigned.

"What do you do for a living, Zalmay?" Jeff asked.

Hamid gave a little chuckle. "I used to be an engineer before the war, now I repair televisions and radios. And I fix cars."

"You have a family?"

"A wife who talks all the time. Four daughters, who follow their mother's footsteps, and three sons. One, the oldest, his name is Saddam." He threw a quick look at Jeff. "I used to be a true servant of Saddam Hussein, but now, with everyone hating him, even though he is dead, not many name their sons *Saddam*."

Jeff chuckled. "As I understand, the name *Adolf* is not as popular as it used to be in Germany."

"Are you German?" Hamid asked.

"No, but my brother-in-law is. He keeps me up-to-date on things like that."

"You have a wife?"

Jeff shook his head. "No. My wife was killed in a car accident ten years ago."

"I am very sorry. It is painful to loose someone you love. I lost two sons. One died shortly before his fifth birthday. He fell ill, but there was no medicine to save him. My other son, my firstborn, he was sixteen when Allah called him home." Again, Hamid glanced at Jeff. "He was killed in a car bombing."

"That is terrible." Jeff felt sorry for the man.

"Yes, it is, especially since he was the only one who died. His car blew up prematurely."

Jeff let that sink in for a second. "Are you telling me your son committed suicide? He was the bomber?"

"That is correct. He became involved with insurgents. After his brother died he became disillusioned with the Americans."

"And you?"

Hamid didn't answer, just concentrated on his driving.

"Me?" he said after a while. "I try to survive as best as I can by working many hours a day to feed my family. I hope it will be better some day."

"It can be," Jeff said, "if your people can put aside their hatred for others of different faiths, and try to be tolerant with each other. This planet is big enough for everyone. Diversity makes it a great place to live on. Stop the bombings, use your energy and money to build up your country, not tear it down. Iraq is the richest oil country in the world, for heaven's sake."

A low chuckle escaped Hamid's throat. "The oil. Yes, that is the magic word. Everybody wants it and everybody wants control of it, especially the big American oil companies."

"Don't give it to them. Let the Iraqis control it, not the foreign oil companies. It is yours, after all."

"You make it sound so simple, my American friend." Hamid sighed audibly. "Life was much easier when I was young. That was before Saddam Hussein. I used to run around in short pants, as did most of my friends. Now, nobody does anymore. There are those who threaten us and our children if we wear western clothing."

"Who are these people who threaten you?"

"Nobody really knows. They just do." He shrugged. "Many Iraqis are dissatisfied with the lifestyle you Americans want to impose on us. They want to go back to the old ways. They want our culture back."

Jeff snorted. "I know, back to the Middle Ages, where women are considered second class citizens, not allowed to be educated. Where they have to cover up their bodies and faces. Where you are persecuted for not believing the doctrines of the day. We left all that behind. We Americans, whom you seem to hate so much, want nothing more for your people than to be free. To throw off the shackles of religion. That's why your government must not be ruled by one religious group but by politicians of different beliefs."

The sound of an explosion nearby made him stop talking, sit up straight and peer out of the window. Then he saw a plume of smoke, saw people running, heard the screaming of wounded and terrorized men and women.

Hamid stopped the car. "Suicide bomber," he commented laconically.

"Another idiot gone," Jeff murmured. "Good riddance! I only hope he didn't murder too many innocent people."

The sirens of an ambulance and the sound of tire-spinning police vehicles added to the pandemonium on the street.

"We need to get moving," Kalila said from the backseat. "We have wasted too much time already on this slow traffic."

"Is there a different route you could use," Jeff asked.

"I know another way, but it could be dangerous," Hamid said.

"Take it!" Jeff told him.

Hamid backed up the car and took a side street. The part of the city they traveled through seemed to be in worse shape than the one they had left. Ghosts of bombed-out buildings lined the streets; pieces of concrete clinging to twisted rods of metal were visible through holes in the walls.

Even the people seemed to be different in their mode of dress and behavior and they looked at their car with open hostility and suspicion in their watchful eyes. They didn't encounter any American soldiers, but many armed citizens that looked like members of a militia.

They had traveled about half an hour, when Hamid slowed down the car and then brought it to a halt.

"Problems?" Jeff asked.

"Not if you do what I ask." Hamid answered. "Do you have any money?"

"Some."

"I hope you brought money. Give me ten thousand dinars."

"Why?"

"Just give it to me!" Hamid said with urgency. "And do not talk, please. Let me do all the talking."

"Give it to him," Kalila said from the back.

Jeff groped around in one of the pockets of the pants he wore underneath his long garment, pulled out a small stack of money and counted out ten thousand dinars. He had barely enough time to put away the rest of the money, when he saw a group of armed men approaching the car.

"Who are those guys?" he asked.

"*Alasas*! Now don't speak!" Hamid said sharply. Then he stuck his head out of the window and called something in Arabic.

One of the men came to his side, while the others circled the car, peering through the dusty windows.

Hamid handed the man the money Jeff gave him, and then he pointed at Jeff, Kalila, and Abduk. After exchanging a few more words, the man outside stepped back and waved them on.

When they were out of earshot, Jeff asked again, "Who were those men?"

"They were *Alasas*. Informants, who watch for outsiders coming into the neighborhood. They do not like nor trust outsiders. I told him, you are my mute cousin from Ramarra coming to celebrate my son's wedding. And your friends in the backseat are my brother and his wife."

"What was the money for?" Jeff asked.

"A bribe. He knew I was lying. You are wearing the wrong clothes for a wedding."

"You're not kidding about the wrong clothes. I wish I could wear a t-shirt and shorts. This damn heat is killing me. I guess you don't have air-conditioning in this car?" Jeff stuck his finger into his collar and shook the front of his dress-like garment, trying to create some air movement against his sweat-covered chest.

Hamid chuckled, not hiding his contempt. "You Americans! You have grown soft with your luxurious cars and homes. That is why you will never win this war with my country."

"We are not at war with your country, not anymore. We are battling a cancer that has infested this part of the world. It is called terrorism. And you people would do well aiding us in this fight. Terrorism must be stopped or it will mean the end of peace for the whole world, yours included, don't ever kid yourself." Jeff felt irritated by the hellish heat torturing his body and the dust making his throat raw and his nose itch. The slow process they seemed to be making didn't help his mood, either. He was anxious to get this whole thing over with and go back home.

They finally left the outskirts of Baghdad and were traveling now at a speed that was not advisable for the road they traveled on. This was a major highway, and Jeff was beginning to wonder what the road to Ash Shatrah was going to be like. Dust billowed up all around them, and when Jeff looked in the rear view mirror, he saw a thick cloud of dust following them.

The heat was stifling inside the car and the wind that rushed by felt like a blast from the fires of hell. They met other cars on the road, some of them occupied by armed men, but nobody paid them any attention.

The countryside looked bleak and rugged, with desert stretching away on both sides, dotted with patches of stunted vegetation, reminding Jeff of Mexico. "What actually grows in Iraq?" he asked the driver, who seemed to be a fountain of information.

"Not very much," Hamid answered. "Mostly date palms. Did you know that eighty percent of the world supply of dates comes from Iraq?"

"I never knew that. Mind you, I'm not really fond of dates." Jeff chuckled, despite the effort it produced in his raw throat. "Unless it's a date with a beautiful woman."

Hamid stayed silent for a moment, and then he laughed. "Oh, I see, you made a joke. A date with a woman. I understand. I never had a date like that."

"You're married to a woman," Jeff said.

"Certainly, but we never had a date. Our marriage was arranged. She is the daughter of my father's brother."

"You married your cousin?"

Hamid nodded. "Oh, yes, that is not unusual. She was lovely and had beautiful teeth when she was young." He gave Jeff a toothless grin. "But that was a long time ago. Now she chews her food with her gums, like me."

"Maybe some day, when things get better, you both can get dentures," Jeff said.

"Maybe." Hamid became silent, just concentrated on the road.

It was close to noon when they saw the outskirts of what Jeff knew to be Al Kut. Hamid decided not to drive through the town and took some back roads that could barely be distinguished from the surrounding desert.

Once they had to wait for a farmer to drive his flock of sheep around them. Hamid greeted him with a few phrases, to which the farmer waved.

Jeff hardly realized it when they finally ended up on the road to Ash Shatrah, and he knew it was going to be a trip through hell, and not just because of the heat. "How long until we get there?" he asked Hamid.

The driver shrugged. "Not long. A little over one hour."

Jeff pulled his pack from under the seat and took out four bottles, offering one to Hamid and handed two bottles to his team members in the backseat. The water tasted brackish and warm, but it quenched the thirst.

The bleak desert-like countryside hadn't changed much. Clumps of brown, withered grass grew from the sand like patches of hair on a mangy coyote. A group of riders on camels moved toward Baghdad, their silhouettes against the bright sun, figures cut out of cardboard, to be pasted into a storybook.

Everything seemed so unreal and surrealistic.

Hamid turned suddenly into a narrow side road. Traveling slower now, they were heading west, toward a row of rugged-looking sand dunes. After cresting a hill, they drove through dry bamboo-like grass, which grew on either side of the road.

The grass became thicker and taller, as they traveled further west. Jeff knew eventually they would encounter one of the tributaries of the Tigris river, which flowed somewhere in the desert, bringing life and hope to the desperate souls who made this dry hell their home.

"This used to be all marsh at one time, but systematic draining and re-routing of the rivers turned it into desert," Hamid explained. "However, it is coming back now."

"Does anyone live here?"

"*The Ma'dan*. Marsh Arabs."

"Is the place we're seeking on this road?"

Hamid nodded. "It is. In fact, we will have to stop now and you must travel on foot."

He brought the car to a halt.

Jeff turned his head to address Kalila and Abduk. "Well, I guess this is it. Let's rock and roll. Make sure your weapons are loaded." He put his hand through the slit in his garment, reached down to his thigh and removed the 9mm Beretta from its holster, checked the fifteen-round magazine and replaced it in its hiding place, satisfied.

If needed, he could draw it fast enough.

He turned to Hamid. "You are certain the people who are holding that little boy hostage are here?"

"Nothing is ever certain." Hamid lifted his shoulders. "According to the information I have, they will be there."

"All right, let's move."

They walked boldly down the road, not exactly knowing what they would encounter. The sun had crept westward, but it still burned with a blazing fire. Jeff inhaled the strange musky smell of decaying vegetation. It reminded him of the times he used to go hunting ducks with Michael.

So long ago but still vivid in his memory. It had never been this hot and the reeds had been much shorter. The only enemy they ever had to face didn't shoot back when flushed out of hiding.

Rounding a corner, they found a number of buildings fabricated entirely from reeds about a hundred meters ahead. A couple of jeep-like vehicles were parked behind the first house. "Well, here goes," Jeff said. He began walking toward the house. Abdul walked beside him and Kalila followed a short distance behind them. As they approached the house, the door opened and a man stepped out. When he spotted them, he stopped and called out something.

Abduk moved ahead of Jeff and said, "As-salam alaykum," to which the other man replied, "Walaykum as-salam."

That was the only thing Jeff understood. When Abduk launched into a string of quick sentences, he didn't understand a word, but he knew what Abduk was saying. *"Our car broke down just a short walk from here. We need help. Perhaps you have a phone we could use to call someone, or you could possibly help us."*

The man in the doorway replied something, and then he indicated for them to come into the house. He stepped aside to let them enter. Jeff followed Abduk, knowing Kalila was close behind.

He heard the door closing, stopped to let Kalila pass him. When he turned, he stared into the muzzle of a gun. Reaching for his own, he stopped when the man said, "Draw your weapon and you're dead."

Jeff realized the man had spoken in English.

He lifted his arms high but didn't say anything, still hoping to bluff his way out of this. The man chuckled and waved his gun. "As-salam alaykum, you American pig. Now move!"

Jeff turned again, saw Kalila and Abduk standing a few feet away from him, their hands in the air. Then he looked at the five men who stood against the opposite wall. Each man held a rifle in his hands.

"Get on your knees!" When Jeff didn't move fast enough, the man behind him kicked him between the shoulder blades with his fist, knocking the wind out of him.

Jeff dropped to his knees, gasping for air. Abduk and Kalila followed his example.

"Now, very carefully, take out your weapons and kick them away from you."

Jeff hesitated for a moment, wondering how fast he could draw his gun and how fast he could shoot the man who held a gun to his head. Not fast enough, he decided. That only happened in movies.

Very slowly to avoid alarming his captors, he reached through the slit in his *dishdashah,* touched the grip of the M9 and eased it out of its holster, suddenly tempted to draw and fire, but when he felt the muzzle of his captor's gun digging into his neck, he aborted that thought.

Pulling out his gun, he pushed it toward the five watching men.

As if waiting for his cue, Abduk and Kalila did the same.

"Good. Now, stretch out and lie on your bellies, keep your faces down and your hands away from your bodies!"

Jeff had barely followed the man's orders, when someone stepped on his right hand. "Tell me, American dog, what are you doing here?"

"Asking for help to fix our broken car."

He groaned when the man increased the pressure of his booted foot on his hand.

"Don't lie to me! I'm asking you again. What are you doing here?"

Jeff decided it was time to tell the truth. "We've come to negotiate the release of the boy."

"What boy?"

"The one you kidnapped and are holding for ransom."

"We know nothing about that."

"Does the name *The Needle of Allah* ring a bell?" Jeff asked.

After a short pause, the man took away his foot. "Who told you about our organization?"

Jeff gave a barking laugh. "Organization? You're a bunch of murderers willing to kill a little innocent boy who has hurt no one. You broadcast it all over your television stations."

"We did no such thing. Those are others who are using our name." He kicked Jeff in the ribs, making him wince and grunt. "This is for calling us murderers. We are freedom fighters. I think you are still lying. You came for something else."

"Nothing else. Just the boy. If you don't have him, who does?"

"Even if I knew, I would not tell you." He spoke a few words in Arabic to his men, and then he said, speaking English again, "Put your hands behind your back!"

Jeff did. He felt rough hands pulling his arms together and someone wrapped a rope around his wrists.

"Now you can sit up."

Jeff rolled onto his side, pulled up his knees and sat up, almost cried out when he felt an agonizing pain stabbing between his shoulder blades where the man had punched him.

I'll kill that son of a bitch if I get the chance!

One of the five men pulled on Kalila's arm, making her stand. She had her face still covered with her shawl and stared defiantly at the man who let them into the house.

"You are dressed like a woman," the man said. "Are you one?" He pulled away Kalila's face covering and let out a sound of surprise.

Kalila said something in Arabic, to which the man laughed. He looked at Jeff. "Is she your whore, American dog?"

Kalila spoke again, sharply. The man hit her across the mouth and shouted a word. Then he turned to Abduk and addressed him on Arabic.

Abduk answered. Obviously, he said the wrong thing because their captor hit him in the belly.

Abduk grunted but didn't cry out. He stood stiffly, looking straight ahead.

Jeff heard the opening door and someone came in. He was not surprised when he heard a familiar voice. The newcomer walked into the room and stood in front of the three captives. Jeff stared at him grimly. "Good to see you in such great spirit, Hamid. I guess you know you won't be getting the bonus I promised you."

Hamid grinned and pulled up Jeff's garment. Then he searched Jeff's pockets until he found the money. Pulling it out, he waved it in front of Jeff's face.

"Don't forget to split that with your friends," Jeff said. "If you would have played it right, you would have gotten much more."

Hamid spit at Jeff. "I want nothing from you, American dog!" He turned and spoke to the other man, who nodded and pointed at Jeff's gun lying in the corner of the room. Hamid walked over to it, picked it up and shoved it into his pocket. Then he looked at Jeff, "I'll use this gun to shoot a few Americans. Maybe even you."

"You don't have the guts to look a man in the eye and shoot him. Why don't you just strap a bomb to your chest, like your son? Wouldn't that be more your style? Allah would be pleased."

Hamid backhanded Jeff. "Do not mock Allah, you filthy American pig!"

Jeff licked his lip, tasted blood and said, "Fuck you!" He strained against the bonds that held his wrists together, wishing he could get his hands free and strangle Hamid.

I should have never trusted this two-faced Allah-worshipping bastard. Should have followed my first instinct. "What are you going to do with us?" he asked the first man, who seemed to be in charge of this little group.

The man shrugged. "Probably kill you. We can't let anyone know about our whereabouts. This is a good place to hide."

Chapter Four

Jeff shifted his position; his left arm was beginning to fall asleep. All their captors had left the house, except for one guard, who sat with his back against the wall, his rifle across his legs.

In the flickering light of the oil lamp, Jeff couldn't see the guard's eyes. He appeared to be sleeping, but Jeff didn't trust his assumption.

"Are you awake?" Kalila whispered beside him.

He could hear her voice clearly, amplified by his earpiece. "Yes, I am," he answered, keeping his voice low.

"We need to escape. They will kill us for certain after sunrise tomorrow morning." Her voice sounded urgent.

"I agree. There is only one problem. I can't get my hands free."

"I managed to slip out of my bonds. Turn and let me untie yours."

Jeff coughed loudly, to see if the guard would look up, but he didn't react. "I think, he's asleep," he whispered. He felt Kalila's hands groping for his, and then she began pulling on the rope. It didn't take long before he felt the rope falling away and he was free.

"Do not move until I untie Sergeant Abduk."

He nodded. Realizing she couldn't see him, he said, "All right," keeping his eyes on the guard, whose head had slumped forward.

"I'm free," Abduk announced with a fierce whisper. "Let me take care of the guard."

Jeff watched Abduk creeping toward the sleeping man. Everything happened in silence and was over in a moment. Abduk rose up beside the man and, with cold efficiency, he grabbed the man's head, twisted it violently and broke his neck. Letting the body slump to the ground, he searched in the man's pockets. Grunting with satisfaction, he produced a gun, shoved it into his own pocket. "I remember him as the one taking it," he commented.

Jeff rose to his feet, rubbed his hands and wrists. Then he went and picked up the rifle, which had slipped from the dead guards hands. He checked the clip and was satisfied to see it full.

Abduk was the first one at the door. He opened it and peered outside. "Looks clear." His voice sounded loud in Jeff's ear, loud enough to wake the whole camp, but he knew Abduk had only whispered. He turned around to throw a last look at the dead guard, feeling a stab of regret for the man's death.

I'm getting soft. It wouldn't have bothered me twenty years ago.

He followed Abduk and Kalila outside, closed the door softly behind him. It seemed bright; the moon was full and threw long eerie shadows across the hard ground. He spotted Hamid's car not far from the house, which meant their driver was still around.

The buildings behind the first house were dark. Everyone seemed to be asleep. He wondered if there was enough time to sabotage the two other vehicles.

Abduk must have had the same thought. "I'll fix them so they can't follow us," he said. Then he ran, crouching, toward the first jeep. He almost reached it, when the door to one of the nearest buildings opened and a man stepped out. Abduk froze but the man spotted him. He called something in Arabic and began walking toward Abduk. While walking, he reached behind his back and pulled out a gun, brought it up to aim it at Abduk.

With a curse, Abduk threw himself to one side, drew his own gun and fired.

The shot sounded loud and unreal in the stillness of the night. Jeff watched the other man fall and cursed, "Shit!" Then he grabbed Kalila's hand and pulled her with him toward the reeds.

A door opened in another building. Two men jumped out, carrying rifles. Abduk shot at them; both men returned fire. Voices shouted inside the houses and then more men spilled into the open.

Jeff and Kalila reached the safety of the reeds. "Sergeant!" Jeff said with a sharp voice. "Get the hell out of there!"

"I think I've been hit," Abduk growled. "Better leave. I'll try to catch up with you."

"Shit!" Jeff cursed again under his breath.

"Our only chance is the marsh." Kalila touched Jeff's arm and pointed. "This way, before they figure it out and try to cut us off."

Jeff followed her, hoping she knew where they were headed. "Abduk?" he called softly. "Are you all right?"

"I'm okay."

His voice sounded strained, and Jeff knew the sergeant wasn't okay. He asked, "Are you safe?"

"For now…but I'm being pursued."

The hammering sound of a machinegun interrupted the silence. Jeff and Kalila dropped to the ground and lay flat, their heads down, but Jeff didn't hear the whining of bullets above them, which meant their pursuers where shooting in a random direction. "They may not know we're here." He looked at the moon, their only way to navigate. "Which way, Kalila?" he asked.

"Toward the moon," she said.

"Sergeant?" Jeff called softly.

"I'm here." Abduk's voice sounded weak. "I heard you. I'll try to make my way in the direction of the moon. We'll meet later."

"How badly are you injured?"

"I'm not sure. I think I'm loosing blood."

"Stay in touch."

"Okay. Signing out. Someone is coming."

It wasn't easy to move through the thick, tall reeds, and the darkness didn't help. They walked in silence, concentrating on the ground beneath them. Jeff could hear voices in the distance, muffled and distorted. He wondered how many men were in pursuit. The ground underneath their feet seemed to become softer, and he found his boots sinking deeper, making walking more difficult. "I want to take a reading," he said and stopped. Pulling out a small compass from a pocked in his pants, he lit up the dial, watched the needle spin gently toward north. "We're heading west. Is that where we want to go?"

"Yes, that is the right direction…toward the river," Kalila whispered.

They moved on, silent again. He didn't hear any more voices. He needed to check up on Abduk. "Sergeant Abduk?"

"Here, Lieutenant."

Jeff had the impression, the voice sounded fainter than before. "I think we're moving apart. You were on our left when we started. Change to Northwest and keep checking your compass."

"All right."

After traveling for about an hour, Jeff heard faint crashing sounds to their left. "Sergeant?"

"Yes, Lieutenant?"

"Do you hear anything to your right?" Jeff deliberately broke a bunch of reeds. They sounded loud in the silence.

"Yes, I do, like someone is breaking something."

"That'll be us, but be on guard anyway. Walk toward us, toward your right." He took the safety off his rifle, held it ready. When he saw the shadowy form of someone moving in the reeds, he asked, "Abduk?"

"It's me, Lieutenant." Abduk joined them a moment later and crouched on the ground, holding his side.

"Let me take a look at your wound, Sergeant," Kalila said.

He waved her off. "There is nothing you can do for me without medical supplies. We have to move on." He rose. "I'm ready."

Jeff checked his compass again. "Where are we actually headed and what are we expecting to find?" he asked Kalila.

"If we can make it to the river, I am hoping to seek help from the *Ma'dan*."

"The Marsh Arabs the driver mentioned?"

"That is correct."

"You're sure they will help us?" Jeff sounded doubtful.

"They are Shi'a, like me. These insurgents are Sunni."

"Okay, then let's get going."

If Abduk suffered from pain, he didn't complain about it. At one time, he handed Kalila his gun. "Here, take this. If we should get surprised, I don't think I'll be able to react fast enough. I need all my energy just to keep up with you."

Kalila took the gun but kept it in her hand. They stopped occasionally to listen, but it seemed their pursuers had given up the chase.

The ground, solid enough until now, gave way to swamp and water. Sometimes they sloshed through water knee-deep. The rays of the rising sun began to wash the top of the reeds with the color of blood, when they finally emerged out of the marsh to find open water. The ground had somehow solidified and they actually stood on some dry land.

Jeff felt exhausted and he could only imagine how Abduk must feel.

"How are you holding out, Sergeant?" Sinking to his haunches, he tried to relax his tired body and regain some strength. He put the rifle beside him, within easy reach. It had been getting heavier with every step.

Abduk smiled crookedly. "To be honest, Lieutenant, I feel like shit."

Jeff could see the dark stain on Abduk's garment. "Perhaps you should let Miss Ahmed have a look at that after all," he suggested.

Abduk nodded and pulled the long dress-like garment over his head, and then he lifted his shirt to expose the left side of his hip. Dark blood crusted most of his skin, with a small trickle of fresh blood oozing out of his wound.

Kalila bent over him and probed the wound with her fingers. "The bullet went straight through. I do not believe it damaged any vital organs. You are lucky, from what I can see, it just missed your hipbone, but you have lost a lot of blood. I would like to clean the area a bit."

She ripped a piece of cloth from the shawl covering her face and went to make it wet. Then she cleaned the blood off Abduk's body, careful not to drip any water into the wound. "Take off your head cloth," she instructed Abduk.

She took it from him and opened it up, and then she wrapped it around his waist. "This might help to stem the flow of blood. Do not move around too much and give the blood a chance to congeal."

Jeff studied the brightening sky. It was hot already and it would be getting hotter as the sun rose higher. The humidity made it feel even more stifling. He'd give a lot right now for those bottles of water in his backpack under Hamid's car.

Hamid! That traitorous son of a bitch!

He watched Kalila finish up with Abduk, remembering Specialist Harmon's concerns about her. "How exactly do you know our driver Hamid?" he asked.

She turned to look at him, her dark eyes thoughtful. "You think I had something to do with the failure of this mission?"

"I didn't say that. I'm just wondering how well you know Hamid."

"I do not know him at all. He is apparently a friend of one of my informers." She shrugged. "I admit, I made a mistake, but time was of the essence. Still is. More so now than ever."

"Well, we didn't find Omar, and I don't believe he was there. Your information was incorrect. It could have cost us our lives. Might still.

We're not safe, yet."

"You are right, Omar was not there, not in the house we were in, nor in any of the other buildings. I should have realized that earlier because the room where they took the video had a brick wall. None of these buildings did."

"Where is he then?"

"Probably in Al Kut. We should have trusted Colonel Settler's intelligence report."

Jeff sighed. "Hindsight is worth nothing. Let's hope we can get back in time to follow that lead." He stared at Abduk, who was lying on his back, his eyes closed. The sergeant's dark skin looked gray. Jeff hoped they could get him to a place soon where he could rest and receive treatment.

His ears suddenly picked up the rustling of reeds and sloshing of water. He reached for his rifle, took off the safety and waited, watching and listening as the noise came closer.

Kalila seemed to have heard it too. She lifted her gun and rose into a half-crouch, ready to check out the commotion. Jeff put a finger against his lips, telling her to stay put. A few moments later two men broke out of the thicket about thirty feet from their position.

Looking around, one of them spotted Jeff and his companions. He shouted and lifted his submachine gun, but Jeff shot him in the chest before he managed to pull the trigger. Beside him, Kalila fired her gun. The second pursuer fell, joined his comrade on the ground. When everything was silent again and no one else appeared, Jeff put down his rifle.

"I guess those two were the only ones."

"It seems that way," Kalila agreed and walked over to the two fallen men, gun still in her hand.

Jeff's eyes followed her. He saw one of the men move, sit up. Kalila lifted her gun and shot him in the head. Then she walked calmly over to the second man, rolled him over with her foot.

Jeff watched this with a slight shudder.

Cold! She's so cold. I don't believe I want to look into her eyes right now.

She bent to search the man. When she came back, she carried the submachine gun, a rifle, and a canteen. "Water," she said. "They do not need it anymore."

Her voice sounded icy, distant. This was not the cuddly, passionate and sensuous woman he had fantasized about in his dreams.

She dropped the weapons onto the ground, opened the stopper of the canteen and took a drink. Then she handed it to Jeff.

The water was warm, but it soothed his parched throat. Giving the canteen back to Kalila, he said, "Let Abduk have the rest. He needs it more than us." Then he grinned. "You wouldn't have some salve I could put on my split and swollen lip?"

"I am afraid not," she said, smiling.

He noticed her lips were as cracked and dry as his. The desert heat makes no distinction between men and women.

Kalila crouched down beside Abduk, who opened his eyes when he heard the shooting. "Did you get them?" he asked, his voice dry and brittle, like the croaking of a bullfrog.

"We did. Here, drink this."

He swallowed eagerly. Kalila touched his forehead. "You are hot. I hope it is just the heat and not an infection."

He smiled up at her. "I'm a tough guy. An American soldier. This is not the first time I've been shot."

"Let us hope it is not the last time." She chuckled. "That did not sound quite right, but you know what I mean."

Jeff sat cross-legged, watching the open water and the shore on the other side. When he spotted a canoe with a lonely occupant coming around a bend in the river, he sat up straight and stared at the slim craft. As it came closer, he noticed the man wore a white shirt-like garment. He had his head-cloth tied loosely around his head. A short mustache adorned his upper lip. Jeff couldn't tell the man's age. He could have been young or middle age.

The man had seen them also and headed his canoe toward them. When he was close, he lifted his hand and called, "Marhaba," to which Kalila replied, "Marhabtayn." Then she began talking rapidly, probably breaking some unspoken law in the process, but this was no time to be too particular about proper protocol.

Jeff didn't understand a word, except for the greeting, which meant 'hello' in Arabic, but he assumed she was pleading for the man's help.

He was right. The newcomer brought his canoe closer to land. Kalila poked Abduk and spoke to him in Arabic. The sergeant sat up, with apparent discomfort, and slowly rose to his feet. He held on to Kalila as he walked to the canoe. He stumbled and almost fell before he reached it, but Jeff jumped forward and caught him.

Kalila spoke again to their new friend. Then she picked up the submachine gun and the rifle, carried both weapons to the canoe and handed them to the man. He took them and stowed them away in front of the canoe. Moving toward the front, he waited until Jeff and Abduk sat safely behind him.

Kalila picked up Jeff's rifle before she climbed into the canoe to sit behind Jeff. "A woman never sits in front of a man," she murmured so low Jeff could barely hear it in his earpiece.

Their rescuer handed Jeff a second paddle, which had been in the front of the canoe, and said something in Arabic. Jeff had no idea what he'd said, but the gesture was unmistakable. He nodded and grabbed the paddle.

Canoeing was nothing new to Jeff and he had no problem paddling. They moved with a good clip, heading to an unknown location.

It didn't matter. As long as it provided safety.

Jeff was tired from the night's ordeal, but he managed to keep up with the younger man. After about half an hour, they arrived at, what looked like, an island. It had several buildings on it in close proximity, similar to the ones the insurgents occupied and, at first, Jeff had the eerie feeling they might have come back to the place of their imprisonment. He saw several canoes and larger boats, fishing vessels by their appearance, moored to the island.

The young man pointed to the island and said something.

"His village," Kalila whispered behind Jeff. "He's going to take us to the Sheik, their leader, who also happens to be his father."

When Jeff climbed out of the canoe and stepped onto the shore, expecting solid land, he discovered it spongy instead. They headed for one of the houses and Jeff found it strange walking on the soft ground; almost like walking on a sparring mat. He saw a few children running around and playing games only they understood. No different from any other village anywhere in the world. A number of women sat in front of their houses, weaving mats or grinding something in large bowls.

Their rescuer took them to one of the houses, where he spoke to the women sitting outside. One of them went into the house and came back a few moments later. Then an old man stepped out, dressed in the long, shirt-like garment typical for Arabs.

Pointing at Jeff's little group, the young man spoke to him. The old man nodded and looked at Jeff. "As-salam alaykum." *Peace be with you.*

Jeff bowed and replied, "Walaykum as-salam." *And to you peace.* He had practiced it long enough. Unfortunately, that was about the extent of his Arabic. When the old man spoke again, Jeff shook his head and pointed at Kalila. She stepped forward and spoke.

The old man was silent for a long time, while Jeff waited patiently. When Kalila finished talking, he smiled and said in perfect Oxford English, "Ah, American. Welcome to my humble home. I am Sheik Khanzir bin Aali bin Tariq Rahman."

Jeff let out a sigh of relief. He made another bow and said, "Thank you for your kindness, Sheik Rahman. My name is Jeff Chartrand. I am asking for shelter and your help. My friend has been shot."

The sheik called back into the house. Two young men came out a few moments later. He pointed to Abduk, who was leaning heavily against Jeff, and gave them an order. They came, grabbed Abduk's arms and led him into the house.

"Please, come," the sheik said, indicating for Jeff to come in.

Kalila said with a low voice, "I will stay with the women. It is their custom."

Jeff followed the sheik into the house. The young men had put Abduk onto a mat on the floor and one was examining Abduk's wound. He said something to the sheik, who nodded. Then the young man went outside to bring back an older woman. She, too, examined the wound. Muttering, she went outside again.

"My wife will take care of your friend. She is very good with medicines," the sheik said. "She has treated gunshot wounds before. We live in violent times." He pointed to a mat. "Sit down and we will talk."

Jeff folded his legs under him, as he lowered his tired body onto the reed mat.

"Tell me what happened. How did your friend get shot?"

Jeff decided to speak the truth, somewhat edited, though. There was nothing to be gained by lying. He told the sheik about the kidnapped little boy, about the kidnappers' demands, and about the betrayal of

Hamid.

The sheik was a good listener, and he never interrupted Jeff once with questions and comments. When Jeff was finished, he said, "I have no love for these insurgents. Most of them are criminals. Who else would use a little boy as a hostage and threaten to kill him? That is not the Muslim way. They use our religion as an excuse to commit murder and other atrocities. I despise them, as do my people, the Ma'dan."

He let out a deep sigh. "My people have lived in these marshes for thousands of years. Our way of life has been the same until the twentieth century, when everything changed. Saddam Hussein drained the marsh, destroyed our villages, our homes, and systematically slaughtered our people. Our numbers used to be in the hundreds of thousands, now we have possibly as few as twenty thousand left. The ones, who have not been murdered, have moved to the cities for what they believe a better life. Many fled to Iran."

He looked at Jeff with a thoughtful expression. "The Americans have freed us from the yoke of Saddam Hussein. Your engineers are trying to bring back the marsh." He smiled sadly. "Of course, it probably is too late for my people. Our life will never be the same. We will help you." He clapped his hands together. "Now we will eat."

They ate in silence. Fish and rice, coarse bread, and they drank sour milk. Jeff was hungry; he didn't care what he ate.

After eating, Jeff asked the sheik, "What do your people do for a living?"

"We fish and we hunt wild boar. We raise water buffalo and grow rice. Our women weave mats from reeds, which we sell at the markets."

"Where did you learn such excellent English?"

The sheik smiled. "I lived in England for five years, when I was a young man."

"Why did you come back to Iraq?"

Sheik Rahman shrugged and took a small sip from his cup. "I did not like the big cities, the hectic life, and the discrimination against people of my race and religion." He waved his hand in a circle. "This is all I need."

Chapter Five

"I told him I am your wife," Kalia said. "Otherwise we would have had to sleep separated. The Ma'dan have very strict rules. Men and women do not eat together, but I made it clear to him that Americans do. Sheik Khanzir bin Aali bin Tariq Rahman is very open-minded."

"His name is quite a mouthful. What does it actually mean?"

"It is a typical Arabian name. It means Khanzir, son of Aali, son of Tariq Rahman."

"Wow. In my country he would be Khanzir Rahman, right?"

"That is correct."

"What about his wife? What names does she go under?"

Kalia chuckled. "Sheik Rahman has more than one wife. A wife does not take on the husband's last name. It is not the custom. Her last name is that of her father. However, the sheik's daughters will bear his last name."

Jeff shook his head. "Sounds complicated to me. Every wife has a different last name. How can you keep it all straight?" He took a sip from his cup and shook himself. "What is this stuff we're drinking?"

"Curdled water-buffalo milk. It is pretty well their staple diet."

"The fish and rice aren't bad, but this...this beverage..." He grimaced and looked around the single room of the house. "These people sure live a primitive life. I can see why the young people want to leave it all behind. Can't say I blame them. They don't even have indoor plumbing."

"No electricity, either."

"And no furniture, except for these mats made from reeds. Whose house is this anyway?"

"It belongs to no one. It is a guesthouse. You have probably noticed that we are on an island?"

"I have. Scary, in a way."

"You may find this hard to believe, but the Ma'dan in all probability built this island from reeds."

"That is hard to believe." Jeff ate some more fish and nodded his approval. "Very good." Licking his fingers, he mused, "I wonder how Abduk is doing? Have you spoken to the sheik's wife?"

"She told me that Abduk is getting better, but he is not fit to travel. He needs rest. She fears his wound will open again and he may bleed to death. He has lost too much blood already."

"We've been here now for two days already. We have to leave." Jeff looked at Kalila, wondering how she managed to look so attractive in her dark dress and without makeup.

She had discarded her scarf, since Ma'dan women did not cover up their faces. He almost wished it were true when she told the sheik they were a married couple. He would be happy to spend a few days with her in this simple house built from reeds. It seemed peaceful here, but he knew that was only an illusion. Nothing had changed in the outside world. They were still holding a little boy named Omar hostage, they still threatened to kill him, unless they had already carried out that threat. The war against terrorism was still on.

As if to confirm it the sound of a jet plane passing overhead interrupted the peaceful silence and brought him back to reality. "We have to leave tomorrow," he said.

"How will we contact the team?" Kalila asked.

Jeff gave her a grim smile. "I suppose you know Rob is a gadget freak? Well, he put a tiny transmitter into the heel of my boot, to be activated if we are in need of rescue. Only to be used under extreme circumstances. We did not expect it to be used."

"And what would classify as *extreme circumstances*?"

"The circumstances we are in, I would say. The problem is, our mission is supposed to be kept low key, for various reasons. I didn't want to come in guns blazing. You of all people should understand that."

"I do," Kalila said, "but we do not have the luxury of playing cloak and dagger games. Not anymore."

"I didn't want these people involved. However, having Abduk injured changes things. He needs to be taken to a place with modern medical facilities and a real doctor." He looked around the room again and smiled. "I'll miss this place. I'll miss your company and these primitive surroundings. Too bad you and I aren't…" He didn't finish the sentence, but he could see by her expression that she knew what he wanted to say.

She smiled almost gently when she looked at him out of her dark expressive eyes. "I also wish things were different," she said softly, "but they are not. I suggest first thing tomorrow you activate that transmitter. Before we do, we have to explain a few things to Sheik Rahman."

* * * *

The helicopter arrived three hours after Jeff activated the transmitter. Black and sleek, it hung like a menacing giant predatory bird at the edge of the island.

Two of the young men from the village brought Abduk on a stretcher, which they had made from reeds. The helicopter could not land on the island. It had to stay in the air, but they lowered a basket and put the sergeant inside. Jeff watched them pull the basket into the belly of the aircraft. He turned and bowed to the old sheik. "Thank you for your hospitality. I don't know how I can repay your kindness."

Sheik Rahman smiled. "The guns and the ammunition you gave me are more than enough." A wicked grin crossed his craggy face. "And the money your friend brought doesn't hurt. It will buy us many things, like medicines and tools. It is my turn to thank you. *Ma'ussalama*, my friend."

"Goodbye to you, also," Jeff said. He walked to the rope ladder and climbed it.

Kalila was already strapped into her seat when he entered the copter.

"I thought you'd never come up, Lieutenant." Rob grinned. "It seems you've made some friends."

"I was tempted to stay," Jeff said, smiling. "These are good people. By the way, how the hell did you manage to get an Apache Helicopter?"

"I had to twist Colonel Settler's arm a little, but I told him it was for a good cause," Rob said, still grinning.

"Well, I'm glad you did. Sergeant Abduk is in bad shape, I'm afraid. He needs medical attention." He strapped himself into his seat, breathing a sigh of relief.

As the helicopter shot across the marsh below, Jeff turned back to Rob. "I guess you've figured out by now our mission has been a failure, so far. That bastard of a driver betrayed us."

"I didn't trust him from the beginning." Rob smiled thinly. "But we'll take care of him later. Right now, our priority is to get back to our command post. Colonel Settler has decided to get involved and provide backup and protection."

The helicopter landed in a park near the hotel, dropped them off and lifted into the air again to take Abduk to a military hospital.

Jeff, Kalila, and Rob walked the short distance to the hotel. Jeff was grateful to find the air conditioning working. Kalila headed straight for the bathroom to take a shower. Jeff decided to talk to the team until she was finished. Even though he felt grimy and filthy, there was nothing else he could do, anyway.

Armano, Hung, and Springer played cards in the living room. They gave Jeff nods of *hello* when he walked into the suite.

"Glad to see you back alive, Lieutenant," Armano said, looking up from his game.

Jeff noticed Harmon in the room with the computers, studying the screens. "Find out anything new?" he asked Rob.

Rob nodded. "I'll show you."

Harmon looked up briefly when he heard them coming into the room and lifted a hand in greeting. Then he went back to his screen.

Jeff observed a highlighted object with a red dot moving slowly across the screen. "Is that our driver?" he asked.

"It is," Harmon answered.

"What about the green dot?"

"That *is* the driver," Rob explained.

"I don't understand."

"Do you still have your gun, Lieutenant?" Rob looked expectantly at Jeff, a tiny smile playing on his lips.

"No, I don't." He suddenly understood. "I see. You put a transmitter into my gun."

"Yes, sir. The fancy grip was just too inviting." Rob gave him a boyish grin. "I figured if things went sour, I could at least get the guy who shot you, Lieutenant. It was not hard to guess he would want your swanky gun."

Jeff shook his head in wonderment. "You're a genius with a devious mind, Rob." His gaze moved back to the screen. "What can we do with this information besides tracking him down?"

"A lot more than appears at first. I think we've located the place where the little boy is held." Rob pointed a finger at a location on the screen. "This is a building in Al Kut. It confirms the information we received from Colonel Settler." He walked over to another screen, did something to the keyboard attached to it. An image zoomed in and Jeff looked at a somewhat blurry picture of a building.

"We believe it is the place where the terrorists are hiding."

"How do you know?"

"We followed your progress up to the point where you entered one of the houses. Here…watch this." His fingers danced again across the keyboard. The scene changed. Jeff saw the somewhat distorted image of a car driving down a narrow dirt road. After the car stopped, three shadows left the car and walked toward a cluster of buildings. One green dot moved with one of the shadows. Once the shadows entered the first building, only the green dot was visible.

"That is your transmitters," Rob explained. "We didn't know what went on inside the house, of course, except that a short time later your transmitter left the house and entered another one. Because the image was not clear enough we had no way of knowing it was the driver and not you."

His fingers moved again over the board. "We didn't know what to make of this, but we had a fair idea that something wasn't right."

Jeff watched as the green dot inside a shadowy figure moved toward the car, entered it. Then the car drove off. This time he saw a green and a red dot. The driver and the car.

"That's when I contacted Colonel Settler. We knew you were in trouble and we waited for your signal, hoping all of you were still alive."

"How did you locate the hiding place of the terrorists?"

"Your driver headed straight for it as soon as he left the other place."

"Son of a bitch!" Jeff swore. "He knew all along where Omar is being held." Stabbing a finger at the screen, he said, "I want that bastard punished!" Then he stared at Rob. "The time for moving stealthily has past. Can we get a military vehicle to take us to Al Kut?"

"I've anticipated your question and I have one standing by. Again, courtesy of Colonel Settler."

"Good. We'll move tonight." He watched the two moving dots on the screen. "Where is he now?"

"He's about twenty miles from Baghdad." Rob studied Jeff with narrow eyes. "What do you think we should do about him, Lieutenant?"

"If I had the chance I'd shoot that traitorous son of a bitch right now!" Jeff said between clenched teeth.

"You want him dead, sir?"

"That's what I said."

Rob turned to Harmon. "You heard the Lieutenant."

"Yes, sir," Harmon said, his fingers flying across his keyboard.

The image of the car zoomed in, became clearer.

"I prepared for this eventuality," Rob said calmly. He walked over to another computer. A third bright dot appeared suddenly on the screen Jeff was watching. It blinked with a steady rhythm.

When the screen lit up brightly, Jeff didn't have to guess what he just witnessed. Staring at the bird's eye view of a burning car, he cursed, "What the hell?" Then he looked at Rob.

"These people love to blow themselves up so they can get to Allah faster," Rob said dryly. "We just helped him along a little."

"You're cold." Jeff shook himself, suddenly thinking of Hamid's family. A wife, four daughters and three sons, now without a husband and father. A man, who had done what he thought best to feed his family. To him, the Americans were the enemy, who invaded his country, bombed the hell out of it, and destroyed his way of life. A life that may not have been perfect but better than the one he had been living now.

He should have worked with us. We would have rewarded him generously. Maybe even allowed him and his family to move to America.

As if reading his thoughts, Rob gave him an inquiring look. "Did I misunderstand, Lieutenant?"

Jeff shook his head. "We gave him a chance, damnit! Why did he have to betray us? He led us there, knowing what would happen to us, knowing he signed our death sentence." He stared at the burning car on the screen. "He had no idea that he also signed his own. Well, what is done is done. I'm going to take a shower. Get the team ready!"

He turned and stalked out of the room. *I can't let feeling like this cloud my mind. I'm a soldier, not a goddamn humanitarian.*

Chapter Six

Driving in the dark was more dangerous than during daylight, but Jeff reasoned the terrorists would be more lax at night, not expecting anyone to drop in for a visit.

Springer, who was the *map-man*, had studied the map of Al Kut and he was reasonably certain he could find the target building even in the dark.

In order not to arouse suspicion and the interest of a lookout, they parked their vehicle on a side street, three blocks away from the house they were seeking. Armano stayed behind to guard the vehicle, while the rest of the team moved under cover of darkness toward their destination.

They split the team to avoid attracting unnecessary attention. Jeff, Rob, and Kalila walked together. Harmon, Hung, and Springer followed a short time later. After locating the two-story building, they took off their black robes, which they had worn over their army fatigues.

Springer, who claimed to have the best throwing arm, hurled a grappling hook onto the roof and clambered up the rope. Once on the roof, he threw down a rope ladder, and the others followed him.

From the satellite surveillance images, they discovered that part of the roof had been destroyed by an explosion. It would allow them entry into the building and lend them an element of surprise.

Jeff, Rob, and Kalila were the first ones to climb through the ragged opening. The room they entered was dark, forcing them to put on their infrared goggles. Rob squeezed himself carefully through the partially open door. One of its hinges had been ripped out of the frame and it made a grating sound as he forced it open.

Jeff and Kalila waited until Rob whispered, "Clear."

Even though he had whispered, it sounded loud in Jeff's earpiece. He and Kalila followed Rob into the corridor. Surveying the long corridor, Jeff saw that most of the doors stood open. Some were gone completely, leaving dark gaping holes in the walls. Only a couple of doors were closed.

Rob eased one open and peered inside, his gun ready. Without a word, he slipped into the room. Jeff and Kalila waited anxiously outside. He came back only a couple of minutes later. It had seemed like an eternity to Jeff.

Rob pushed a man ahead of him. The man's mouth was covered with his own headpiece. Pulling the man's arms tightly together behind his back, Rob used a tie wrap to bind his wrists. Then he dragged him into one of the empty rooms at the far end of the corridor.

The door seemed intact, and Jeff managed to close it.

"Ask him where the boy is," Rob told Kalila. The captive's face looked gray in the beam of Rob's flashlight.

Jeff pushed up his goggles and turned on his headlamp. Kalila bent down and spoke to the man in a low voice.

He shook his head and grunted something.

"What is he saying?" Rob asked.

"He cannot talk with his mouth covered up," Kalila whispered.

"Take it off then but tell him I'll shoot him if he starts to yell."

Kalila translated what Rob had told her. The man nodded and she removed the cloth from his mouth. Then she asked him again.

Their captive spoke a few words in his native tongue.

"Well?" Rob stared at her. He had his goggles pushed up onto his forehead, but he didn't switch on his headlamp, just kept the beam from his flashlight in the man's face.

"He does not know what we are talking about."

Rob walked up to the man and shoved the barrel of his gun into one of his nostrils. "Talk, you son of a bitch!" he cursed through clenched teeth, his voice a loud hiss.

The man struggled and Rob kicked him in the ribs with his booted foot. "Tell him he'd better talk! We don't have time to play twenty questions and answers."

Kalila spoke again, but their captive shook his head and spat out a few words.

"I'll be back," Rob told Jeff and handed him his flashlight.

Jeff nodded, strangely detached from this whole situation. He looked down at the flashlight in his hands and then at the bearded face of the man cowering on the floor, his eyes squinting against the glare of the light.

It didn't take long for Rob to return. He pushed another struggling man ahead of him, also bound and gagged. "I brought a friend," he said to the man on the floor, even though he knew he wasn't understood. "Ask our new friend here the same question," he told Kalila.

The newcomer was as co-operative as the first one. Rob hit him once across the mouth, splitting his lips. "Tell them, one of them better talk. My patience is running out," Rob snarled.

Deep down Jeff was appalled by Rob's conduct, but he knew that it was necessary. He had played similar games twenty years ago. He also knew what would come next. He did nothing to stop it. A little boy's life was at stake, and these men were criminals in his eyes. They didn't deserve any mercy.

Kalila spoke to the men again, but they denied any knowledge of the boy.

"Is it possible they really don't know? Are you sure we're in the right building?" Jeff asked, doubt creeping up inside him.

Rob chuckled grimly. "This is the right place. We saw armed men coming out of it, and your late friend Hamid was here to warn them."

He pulled his combat knife from its sheath and put the sharp edge against their first prisoner's throat. "Tell him I'll send his comrade to *Allah-land* if I don't get an immediate answer. Ask him in which room the boy is being held."

Kalila translated again. The man she spoke to spat at her and uttered a string of sharp syllables.

"What did he say?"

"He says *Whoso slayeth a believer of set purpose, his reward is hell forever. Allah is wroth against him and He hath cursed him and prepared for him an awful doom.*"

"Wow! In other words, he is telling me to go to hell. Unfortunately for him, he is not in a position to threaten me. Ask the other guy."

After Kalila repeated the question, the man with the knife to his throat also spat and spoke rapidly.

"I have a feeling I'm not going to like his answer, either," Rob said, "but tell me anyway."

"Allah is great and will not allow an infidel to take the life of one of his devoted followers."

"Really?" Rob chuckled. "Then tell him to say hello to Allah from me." He spoke calmly and stepped behind the prisoner.

Kalila stared at him for a second and then she translated.

The man's eyes grew wide, he opened his mouth to speak, but his words were cut off, when Rob, almost casually, pulled back his head and drew his knife across the exposed throat. A stream of crimson spurted out of the gaping cleft. The man's body jerked and his feet kicked violently as Rob let him slide to the ground.

Jeff felt like being sick, repulsed by the casualness of the way Rob had taken a life. "Fuck it!" his mind screamed. *Why must there be all this violence? I want this to end!*

Rob gave the limp body a kick with his foot. "Tell him he'll join his friend in Hell unless he talks."

Kalila spoke slowly, her voice cool and calm, as if what just had taken place didn't affect her. Jeff remembered how she had shot one of the two insurgents in the marsh, remembered the chill in her voice after shooting him in the head in cold blood, without so much as the slightest bit of hesitation.

No, she was not affected.

He watched her as she drew her own gun and put it against the second prisoner's temple. The man struggled against his bonds, but then he spoke with a low voice. Kalila put away her gun.

"The boy is in a room downstairs. It faces the back of the building. The third door after we come down the stairs."

"How many men are guarding him?"

After putting the question to the man, she said, "Three."

"Ask him, how many men in this building?"

At first, the man seemed to hesitate, but when Kalila aimed the gun at his kneecap, he answered.

"Fifteen, excluding him and the man you murdered."

"Executed, not murdered," Rob murmured and stared at the captive. "How many on this floor?"

"Five in the other room," Kalila said after the man answered.

"Good. That means ten downstairs. We can handle that." He looked at Jeff. "What do you think, Lieutenant?"

The fact that Rob addressed him surprised Jeff. "What do you want to hear?" he asked.

"How do you want to proceed?"

Jeff had the feeling Rob was just humoring him. So far, he had been the one in command.

Probably still was.

"What do you suggest, Specialist Masters?" he asked, trying to save face.

"I suggest we let Team Beta take care of the insurgents on this floor, while we rescue the boy."

"I agree." Jeff nodded. "Tell Team Beta to join us."

Jeff knew it wasn't necessary, because the men had been listening in on their communicators. Rob walked to the door and opened it. Harmon, Hung, and Springer joined them a few moments later.

"You know what to do," Rob told them and pointed at the captive. "Treat him well. He was quite helpful."

"Let's go," Jeff said. He pushed his goggles back over his eyes and left the room, trying to show some initiative. Rob and Kalila were close behind him as he carefully climbed down the stairs. The third door toward the back, he told himself. *Let's hope the information is correct.*

He became suddenly aware of the acrid smell in the building, of the cooking odors mixed with urine and other, unidentifiable, scents. None of them pleasant. The smell of death seemed to ooze from the walls; they were damp and the air within these cement walls was humid and hot. Jeff felt clammy inside his clothing.

As he stepped down from the last step onto the tiled floor, a door further down the corridor opened and a man, carrying a lantern, stepped out.

Jeff froze. He sensed Kalila beside him, motionless, and Rob a few steps behind them. The man came walking toward them, obviously oblivious to their presence. He may never have noticed them, except for the fact that his destination was the staircase. When he was about ten feet away, he looked up and spotted them.

He stopped in his tracks, his eyes narrow as he stared at them over his lantern. Then he seemed to realize they were not members of his group but intruders.

He shouted a word and turned to run. Jeff acted without conscious thought. With a swift, practiced motion, his fingers curled around the hilt of his combat knife, pulled it free and sent it hurtling after the fleeing man. Seven inches of polished steel found its mark, buried itself between the man's shoulder blades. He stumbled, fell but managed to utter a gurgling scream. His lantern went flying, the glass shattered and oil spilled across the broken tiles. The flames spread and lit up the darkness.

Jeff pushed up his goggles, registered Rob opening the first door and throwing something inside. Kalila did the same with the door to her right.

He heard shouts coming from that room, and then an explosion shattered the silence, followed by another one from Rob's room.

"Second floor secured." Harmon's voice erupted from the speaker in Jeff's ear.

"Team Beta, combat situation on first floor," Jeff said sharply. "On the double!"

Kalila had already moved to the next door on her side, while Rob took the second one on their left, skirting the burning flames on the floor. Jeff coughed when he inhaled the choking fumes. He bent to pull his knife out of the dead man's back, pushed it into its sheath, heading for the third door.

Looking back, he saw the three men from Team Beta bounding down the stairs, weapons ready. "Secure the other rooms!" He spoke a sharp order. "Kalila, you come with me!"

He felt cold and calm inside. His body and mind had finally shifted into combat mode. Just before he reached the door, it opened and a man stuck out his head. Jeff reached out and grabbed the man by the collar, yanking him out of the doorway. Then he threw him across the corridor, right into Rob's arms.

He kicked open the door. The time for stealth had long passed. He held his gun in one hand and his flashlight in the other. The beam of his light fell upon a scene he had desperately tried to keep out of his mind.

Against the far wall, beside a small table that held a burning lantern, stood a man and a little boy. The knife in the man's hand gleamed dully as he held the keen blade against the throat of the boy.

Omar! Jeff would have recognized him anywhere.

The man holding the knife had pulled a black mask over his face. "One step closer and the boy is dead," he warned in perfect American.

Jeff thought he detected a southern accent. "Don't make a stupid mistake," he told the man. "You kill the boy and I'll put a bullet into your head. Let him go and you might just live."

The man laughed. "I *might* live? That's not good enough."

"What would be good enough?"

"One million American dollars in a Swiss bank account for one thing."

"And the other thing?"

"Keeping my identity a secret."

"I assume you're not an Iraqi, right? Possibly an American?"

"I'm not answering that, and don't start guessing."

Jeff looked around the room. He recognized it as the one he had seen in the video. In one corner, he saw a video camera on a tripod. In the other stood four army cots. Thin blankets lay on all of them.

He was searching for the third man who was supposed to be in the room. Rob seemed to have the same idea because he did a slow sweep with his flashlight, locating the man crouching behind one of the cots.

"Tell your accomplice to get up and start walking toward us with his hands in the air," Rob told the masked man, who relayed the message to the man cowering on the floor.

He didn't get up but uttered a few words.

"He wants to have your assurance you won't shoot him."

"As long as he is unarmed he has nothing to fear," Rob said.

The man with the mask forwarded the message again and the other man rose slowly, lifting his hands. Then he came around the cot and walked toward them.

When the masked man spoke again, Kalila yelled something in Arabic and brought up her gun. "He's got a bomb strapped to him!"

The man kept on walking. Kalila shouted again. Jeff was watching the man with the knife, his eyes on the blade touching the boy's jugular. He didn't dare looking into the boy's eyes, large with fright. His nerves were as taut as a bowstring, but he felt curiously calm and cool.

Like a detached observer.

Then everything happened at once. The explosive sounds of shots fired in the corridor outside gave him the chance he had waited for; beside him shots fell. He knew it was Kalila. The man who held the boy moved the knife away from the boy's throat for a fraction of a second. Squeezing the trigger of his gun, Jeff was painfully aware there was no room for mistakes.

He heard Rob firing his gun at the same time as he did.

His system fuelled by adrenalin, he raced across the room toward the boy and the man who, almost in slow motion, began to topple backward. Reaching the pair, Jeff pushed the boy away from the hovering knife, gathered him up in his arms. The boy uttered a loud scream, struggled against him, his little fists pummeling his shoulder.

"It's all right," Jeff said soothingly. "You're safe."

Then Kalila was beside him, spoke to the boy in Arabic. The boy stopped struggling, but his little body was racked by uncontrollable sobs.

"Give him to me," Kalila said gently. Jeff handed her the boy. He heard her utter crooning words.

She has softness inside and compassion. Not the cold bitch I thought she was, after all. The thoughts popped into his mind as his eyes searched the door where Rob stood, his gun still in his hand.

"Building secure." Harmon's words sounded harsh in his ear.

He holstered his gun, felt his body relax.

"It's over, Lieutenant," Rob said, holstering his own gun.

Jeff looked at the masked man on the floor. He was tempted to take off the mask and look into the face of a man who was willing to murder a little boy for a million dollars. Staring at the pool of blood beside the hooded head, he shrugged. It didn't really matter. As far as he was concerned, the man was a criminal who played the role of a terrorist.

A nobody!

He wasn't going to make him famous in his death.

Walking up to the table, he took a second lantern and poured the oil over the corpse. Then he threw the burning lantern on top of it. Flames shot up as the oil ignited and began licking at the still body.

"Burn, you son of a bitch! Just as your soul will burn in hell. You weren't even man enough to show your face," Jeff cursed. He turned away, feeling coldness and at the same time sadness inside him…and emptiness. To take another man's life is never a pleasant thing, but this man didn't deserve to live. He was a criminal and a coward. A quote from Shakespeare popped into his mind. *Cowards die many times before their deaths; the valiant never taste of death but once. Of all the wonders that I yet have heard, it seems to me most strange that men should fear; seeing that death, a necessary end, will come when it will come.*

He was surprised he remembered it. He also remembered it was a quote from Julius Caesar.

Throwing one last glance at the burning body, he turned to Harmon. "What about the rest of the terrorists?"

"All of them are dead, sir."

"All?"

"Yes."

He wasn't surprised. There was no mercy in these young men. They were trained killers. *So am I. I am no different from them!*

Armano picked them up in front of the building. The street outside was dark. Nobody seemed to have noticed the battle inside the building.

Maybe nobody cared.

Chapter Seven

They took Omar to the military base. From there a transport plane would take him to the US and safely deliver him to Jeff's sister.

Colonel Settler assured him there'd be no problems. "Your mission is not in any files and as far as anyone is concerned, the boy was murdered by the kidnappers. There will be no paper trail connecting Omar to these terrorists."

When he walked out of Colonel Settler's office, Rob met him and said, "We still have to tie up some loose ends. One more mission."

"When?"

"Tonight."

"Who gave the orders?"

Rob smiled thinly. "Standing orders from Colonel Crowley, to be used at my discretion. We also have Colonel Settler's blessing."

Jeff didn't question it and when he sat in the Apache helicopter, he could almost guess the matter of the mission. They flew under cover of darkness. When they reached their destination, he was not surprised to recognize the cluster of buildings on the screen. The images of men walking among them were displayed in white, as were the five vehicles parked between the houses.

"We're in luck," Rob told Jeff. "It seems they're getting ready for something. See the weapons they're loading onto their vehicles?"

Jeff nodded, knowing what was going to happen next.

"Take them out!" Rob ordered the gunner.

The hammering of the rocket launcher shattered the silence, followed by a number of explosions on the screen.

Jeff didn't hear the screams of the dying men. A few of them crawled on the rocky ground toward the illusive safety of their vehicles, trying to flee the sudden death raining down upon them from the sky, but safety was not to be found. The vehicles exploded, the ammunition stored inside them creating a spectacular fireworks display. Deadly and destructive in its terrible beauty. The reed houses burst into flames that lit up the night.

"I believe our work here is done," Rob said matter-of-factly.

"I guess it is," Jeff agreed, wondering how many of the insurgents they had killed. How much of a dent had they made in the fight against terrorism? There seemed to be an endless supply of new recruits…young men willing and eager to die for their cause and their god, hoping to collect a reward for murdering innocent men, women, and children.

He would never be able to figure out such twisted logic.

They didn't talk much on the way back to the military base. Settler was happy when they reported the success of the mission. "The terrorist cell which calls itself 'The Needle of Allah' is not unknown to us," he told Jeff. Then he handed him an envelope. "Here are your new orders, Lieutenant Chartrand. For you and your team."

Jeff gave the colonel a perplexed look. "Aren't we going home?"

"I'm afraid not." Settler paused. "I've had these orders on my desk ever since you arrived. Colonel Cowley asked me to wait until you accomplished your mission. Rescuing that little boy was only part of your job here."

Jeff grimaced. "Why am I not surprised? I always wondered why Colonel Cowley would go to all this effort and expense just to save the life of a foreign unimportant child."

"It doesn't sound very charitable when you say it like that." Settler gave him a little smile. "It is true, Colonel Cowley had ulterior motives, but his orders came from higher up."

"What are we supposed to do?"

"The terrorist group 'The Needle of Allah' has been buying weapons from unscrupulous arms dealers in the US. We have information that a deal is going down three days from today. Your job is to intercept the insurgents and take their place. We want to get at the dealers back home. Stop them at the source."

"You don't know who they are?"

Settler shook his head. "No, we don't. They are smart, illusive, and well organized, using a layer of middlemen and companies to do their dirty business. The men who are delivering the weapons are usually military personnel currently in service or ex-military men and mercenaries."

* * * *

Timing was everything. They had to take out the insurgents before the weapons were delivered and then meet with the arms dealers.

Jeff had no illusions about the mission. Taking out the insurgents might not be too difficult, but dealing with the men delivering the weapons would be extremely dangerous. It didn't matter if they were soldiers or mercenaries. They'd be wary and cautious. If they suspected something wrong, they would fight to the death, showing no mercy. They could not afford mercy. There could not be any witnesses.

However, Jeff believed in his team. Too bad, they'd be one man short. Sergeant Abduk would have contributed greatly to the success of this mission.

When Kalila told him she'd be part of the team, he didn't know if he should be happy about her decision. He still didn't trust her fully, since he didn't really know anything about her, except for the stuff she'd told him.

She certainly was capable. She proved that, but there was the incident with the driver Hamid. How could she have been so neglectful and not have him checked out?

Rob and the others didn't say much when he told them about Kalila's decision.

"Maybe it'll be a good thing," Rob commented. "With the Sergeant gone, we don't have anyone who speaks Arabic. She might be useful."

Jeff looked at Harmon. "No other concerns?"

Harmon shrugged. "I'll still be watching her."

"Very well then, gentlemen. Get a good night's rest because tomorrow night we'll be going into action."

They had given up their rooms in the hotel in Baghdad and moved into the barracks with the enlisted men. If the other soldiers knew that the newcomers were not regular army, they didn't comment or ask questions.

Kalila arrived at the base the next day. Jeff didn't ask her where she'd been. He hoped she'd tell him if she thought it was necessary for him to know.

Their destination lay northeast, toward the Iranian border. They left shortly after lunch in a couple of battered vehicles, dressed in local garb thrown over their regular outfits.

This time, they carried pistols, M-16s, and plenty of ammunition.

When Jeff looked at the vehicles for the first time, he protested, worried they might break down and leave them stranded in the desert. The mechanic in charge put his worries to rest and assured him that they were in excellent condition, with rebuilt motors and transmissions.

"Better than new," he said, grinning.

Jeff split up the team again. Rob sat behind the wheel and he in the passenger seat, with Kalila and Master Sergeant Suliman in the backseat.

Suliman was a last minute addition to the team, courtesy of Colonel Settler. He spoke Arabic like a native. They would need him to communicate with the arms dealers, who might get suspicious if they dealt with someone who spoke American without an Arabic accent. Kalila would not do because she was a woman, even though she wore men's garb and had glued on a false mustache. A headpiece hid her long hair. Good enough for visual inspection, but her voice would give her away.

All of them studied the maps and surveillance photos; however, the vehicle with Springer took the lead, since he was the map-reader.

Colonel Settler provided them with a military escort vehicle displaying a rocket launcher. They didn't have the time to deal with 'neighborhood governments'. It took them through Baghdad. Once they reached the outskirts of Baghdad they were on their own. Part of the journey, they traveled on a highway that led north to Ba'qubah, but before they reached that city, they took a side road heading east.

It was another hot day and the new road they traveled didn't make it any easier. Clouds of dust swirled up behind the lead vehicle and they had to leave more distance between the two vehicles than Jeff would have liked in order to see the road and avoid inhaling too much dust.

The terrible heat forced them to drive with their windows half-open, and soon a coating of dust covered the inside of the car. Jeff followed Kalila's example and wrapped part of his headpiece over his mouth.

"We should have brought facemasks, damnit!" he cursed.

Before long, he was drenched in perspiration, and he knew the others didn't fare any better.

"Didn't you tell me that the Garden of Eden was once located in Iraq?" He turned his head to look at Kalila.

"So the legends tell us."

"Well, those legends are wrong. I think it was Hell, not the Garden of Eden. In fact, I believe this is still Hell. The heat, the dust, the hatred and violence all around us. How can it be anything else? It certainly isn't Paradise."

"No, it is not," she agreed. "Not anymore."

They were silent for the rest of the trip. Rob concentrated on his driving, careful not to hit the small boulders and rocks littering the road. They encountered little traffic, except for the occasional sheepherder. When they came to a river, the first vehicle stopped and one of the men got out inspecting the bridge that led across it. He waved to the second vehicle and then he climbed back into his car. They drove slowly, one vehicle at a time, and Jeff breathed a sigh of relief when they reached the other side.

The road didn't improve after that. The first car stopped again and waited until Jeff's vehicle caught up.

"According to this map, we are about one mile from the insurgent group," Springer told them. "It should be right behind that hill."

"Good. We'll wait until dark and then we'll move in." Jeff surveyed the surrounding area, and then he glanced at the setting sun. "There is not much cover. We have to rely on the darkness to aid us in sneaking up on them. Once in the camp, show no mercy. Kill them all. Understood?"

"Understood, sir." The men nodded in agreement.

Jeff looked at Kalila. "Any second thoughts?"

She shook her head. "None."

He knew it sounded so easy, *Just move in and shoot everyone in sight*, but he knew it wouldn't be that easy. Any one of them might die tonight. Possibly all.

"Check it out," he told Rob.

Rob ran up the hill, crouched as he neared the top. He dropped to the ground and crawled on his belly the rest of the way. Jeff saw him looking through his field glasses. After a few minutes, Rob came back with a tiny smile on his face.

"Piece of cake," he said. "There are only two buildings and three sheds, with a couple of trucks parked in the front. I don't believe there are more than eight people in those houses."

"Any sentries?"

65

"None that I could see. I don't think they suspect anything. Not way out here in this desolate place."

"We can't assume that, but you are probably correct." Jeff rubbed his beard. His skin felt itchy and his lips dry. He wished for a cold drink, preferable a bottle of beer...and a shower! None of them available right now. "It will be dark within the hour," he said. "We should get ready."

The men removed their outer garments. They'd be able to move more stealthily without them. Aside from the fact those dresses were white and not exactly the perfect clothing for hiding in the dark.

Rob and Springer checked their backpacks, which contained a number of grenades. The others made sure they had full magazines in their pistols and M-16s.

Darkness fell swiftly and the men started moving toward the hill. The moon was still hidden behind the mountains in the east. Jeff knew they had possibly one hour until it would make its appearance. By then everything should be over.

It took them less then twenty minutes to reach the houses. As they came closer, they heard the chattering of a generator, making it that much easier to get close without worrying about making too much noise.

Diffused light shone through small windows, evident that both houses were occupied.

The men spread out as they came near the houses. Jeff pointed to Springer and then at the second house and whispered, "Team Beta. Target number two."

Springer nodded, and he, Harmon, Hung, and Armano headed for the second house, while Kalila, Suliman, and Rob joined Jeff to take out the insurgents in the first building.

"On my mark," he whispered. He wanted Springer and Rob to be the first ones to bust through their doors and throw a couple of grenades into the rooms.

"Go!"

Rob kicked open the door and threw in the first grenade, followed it with a second before he jumped back and out of the way.

The explosions rocked both houses at the same time. The men waited outside the door, weapons ready, but nothing moved inside the house. A series of shots from the back of the other house made Jeff look around. "Report!" he said sharply.

"One of them tried to leave through a window in the back." Jeff recognized Hung's voice. "He's been eliminated." Hung's voice sounded dispassionate, distant.

"Check out the inside of the buildings but be cautious."

They didn't find anyone alive. Jeff counted six bodies.

"No survivors," Springer reported from the other house.

"How many men inside?"

"Five."

That made twelve casualties. Jeff relaxed. In a way, the assault had been anti-climactic. Almost too easy but not unexpectedly so. The two grenades created havoc inside the room. Remnants of a computer lay in one corner, together with pieces of a desk. There wasn't much left of the dead body in front of it. One of the grenades must have exploded right beside him.

The explosion tore up the other bodies almost as badly. Identification would be difficult, something Jeff didn't really worry about.

Amazingly, the single light in the ceiling was untouched and still burning.

A couple of rooms in the back were empty, except for sleeping blankets and prayer carpets. They also found some food bundled up in cloths.

Springer and his team came to join them. "Looks like we've stumbled across one of their main camps," he said. "There is a sophisticated satellite broadcasting system in the other house. Unfortunately, most of it was destroyed by the grenades."

"Let's clean up the mess," Jeff said. "Harmon, Hung, you two load the bodies and what's left of them onto one of the trucks and drive it into the desert, away from here. In this heat, they'll decompose fast and we won't be able to breathe by tomorrow. Springer, Suliman, and Armano, take the other vehicle and bring back our cars. We can't leave them on the road."

The discovery of a metal box containing two million dollars in crisp one hundred dollar bills confirmed they had the right place.

"I'll bet my right arm that this money is counterfeit," Rob said.

Jeff agreed. "We can't let this money reach the United States."

Chapter Eight

They spent the night sleeping in the first house, but not before they moved all the blankets and rugs into the other house. The men slept in one of the rooms and Kalila in the other one.

Breakfast consisted of rations they brought with them.

After breakfast, Hung and Springer checked out the sheds. "They're empty, except for a bunch of containers filled with gasoline," Hung reported.

"We can use the gasoline," Jeff said. "No sense letting it go to waste."

The rest of the day they waited, dressed in the long white shirt-like garments. However, Jeff didn't think the arms dealers would show up before dark, because deals like that were accomplished best under cover of darkness. It was the nature of things like that.

Those people would be suspicious beyond reason and worry about being spotted, especially these days when the attention of spy satellites was focused on the Middle East.

Spy planes would be another danger they'd worry about.

Jeff was quite certain they would not make an appearance during the day. Even though, he had Hung keep a lookout for any unexpected visitors.

His assumption was correct. It was dark when Hung came bounding back to the camp. They heard the soft rumbling of the trucks before they saw the headlights. When they crested the hill, Jeff counted three army trucks and one jeep.

They'd parked the one remaining truck of the insurgents and their own cars further down the road, not easily visible, unless someone looked for them. Floodlights over the doors lighted up the space in front of the houses

As if on cue, Suliman stepped outside when the vehicles pulled up.

Jeff joined Suliman on the doorstep, an M-16 casually dangling in his hands.

Armano and Hung were hiding in one of the sheds, watchful for possible hostilities their visitors might display. Kalila stayed in the darkened house, by the window, while Springer did the same in the other house.

When the trucks rumbled to a halt, Rob stepped out of the door of the other house. Suliman walked toward the jeep, his hands empty to show that he was unarmed.

A couple of men in army fatigues jumped out of the jeep. Jeff stood close enough to see the thin mustache on one of the soldier's lips. He could have been Rob's taller brother. The resemblance was uncanny.

"Asalamaleikum," Suliman greeted them. He held out a hand. "Welcome."

The one with the mustache eyed him, ignoring the outstretched hand. "Are you the guy in charge?"

Suliman chuckled. "I am the negotiator."

"Where is Hassan?"

"He is absent. He gave me full authority to deal with you."

Jeff was somewhat surprised at Suliman's heavy Arabian accent. He couldn't have been more convincing.

"Okay. Show me the money first."

Suliman lifted a hand. Springer came out of the other house, carrying the metal box. He brought it over, set it down and flicked open the lid.

The soldier stared at the contents. "Do I have to count it?"

"Go ahead if you don't trust us. There are two million American dollars in there." Suliman looked at the soldier. "Now let me see your merchandise."

The soldier signaled to the first truck. The driver of that truck pulled ahead, parked it beside the jeep. Another soldier jumped out of the passenger's side and walked to the back of the truck, where he lifted the back flap.

Jeff joined Suliman to make his own inspection. Suliman asked, "What's in the boxes?"

The soldier with the mustache gave a small chuckle. "Whatever you ordered, my friend." He pointed at one of the boxes. "A couple of rocket launchers." His hand moved. "Grenades. Be careful with those. Don't blow yourself up before we leave. That other box behind it is full of handguns. Fifty M-1911s. Only the best for our customers. Plenty of clips in the other boxes."

"Where are the machine guns?"

"Impatient, aren't we?" The soldier laughed. "You may have noticed there are two more trucks. The machine guns and the rifles are in one of them."

"And what is in the other truck?"

"Ah, I knew you'd be anxious to find out, my friend. Come with me and I will show you." The soldier spoke jovial and gave Suliman a friendly clap on the shoulder. "A surprise." He laughed as if he had told a joke.

Jeff felt suddenly weary. He didn't have a good feeling about this.

The soldier who had thrown back the flap of the first truck joined in on the laughter. Jeff saw him touching his sidearm and hung back a little as he followed the three men. He had seen the tiny earphone sticking out of the men's ears and he knew they communicated with other soldiers, who were still out of sight.

"I smell a rat," he whispered into his own comm., alerting his men.

Suliman put his hand into a slit in his garment in a casual gesture. Jeff knew Rob was watching and also knew he could count on Kalila, who was probably keeping the sights of her rifle aimed at the man by the jeep. From the corner of his eye, he saw Springer moving into position, watching the driver in the first truck.

"By the way," the soldier with the mustache said, casually, "you've got quite a nice setup here. How many people in your little group?"

Suliman waved his free hand. "There's us, the ones you see, and then there are the ten in the house who are busy saying their prayers."

"In the dark?" the soldier asked, suspicion creeping into his voice.

"We prefer it that way. It is not really that dark in the room. You'd be surprised how much light a candle can produce."

"Ten men, eh?" The soldier turned to look at his comrade. "Did you hear that, Drummer? Quite a nice little group, don't you think so?"

"Sure is. Quite a nice group." Drummer chuckled. "And all of them praying. They might just need it, hey Serge?"

The one called *Serge* turned back to Suliman. "All in one house?"

"Yes, in the other house."

"The other house. Hmm…"

The second truck began to move suddenly and the driver turned it around, the back toward the second house. When Drummer saw Suliman watching the truck, he said, "Just putting it in position so your men can start unloading it as soon as they're finished praying."

They reached the rear of the third truck. "What is the surprise?" Suliman asked.

"This!" the soldier said, drawing his sidearm.

"I wouldn't do that!" Suliman advised him, dropping his phony accent. The gun in his hand underlined his warning.

Jeff had been watching Drummer, who managed to draw his pistol from its holster.

"Jeff, behind you!" Kalila's anxious voice sounded like a scream in his ear and he swung around, bringing up his M-16. Another soldier had climbed out of the third truck, unnoticed by him. He had a gun in his hand, pointed at Jeff.

There was no time to think about anything. Jeff fired a short burst, saw the man drop. He heard a shot nearby. A heavy body fell beside him. He realized it must be Drummer doing the shooting.

"Fucking camel drivers!" screamed a voice. Another shot ripped through the silence of the night.

Things seemed to happen all at once. The cover of the second truck was thrown back, revealing a soldier with a rocket launcher, aimed at the house. Two soldiers with submachine guns jumped to the ground. A flame shot out of the back of the launcher. Jeff heard the thunder of an explosion and then he saw flames lighting up the night from the spot where the second house once stood.

One of the soldiers from the truck didn't get far. He sprawled onto the dusty ground, his submachine gun sailing across the dirt. His companion looked around for a target, fired a round at the house Kalila was hiding in. He fell when Jeff shot him.

Looking at the cab of the truck beside him, Jeff saw a soldier slumped over the wheel. Then he saw Armano and Hung coming out of the shed in a crouching run, easily visible in the headlights of one of the trucks. They had discarded their native garb.

"Get down!" someone shouted. They both dropped, rolled away like two rolling pins. Jeff did the same, his training taking over his body. He saw the cover of the third truck pushed up, saw the row of rifle barrels flashing in the glare of the floodlights.

"Don't even think about it!" he yelled, his M-16 covering the soldiers peering anxiously around them, temporarily blinded by the light.

"Get off the fucking truck!"

Jeff was glad to hear Suliman's voice. Glancing down, he saw the body of the man called *Serge* lying unmoving on the ground. Jeff rose, his weapon aimed at the soldiers, who sat as if petrified. "Throw down your rifles first!" he ordered them.

They complied, reluctantly, it seemed. Then they climbed off the truck. He counted five men, all of them young. "Check the cabs!" he told Armano and Hung, who had risen from their places on the ground.

"Bring the prisoners into the light," he told everyone.

In addition to the five from the third truck, the men brought six more captives. Even though they all wore American outfits, Jeff wondered if they were actually American soldiers.

"How many of you are Americans?" He looked them over and stared at the last prisoner who was being propelled forward by Rob.

"I found this one in one of the trucks," Rob said. "He pretended to be dead."

"I had a feeling we'd meet again," Jeff said, "but I didn't think it would be here. Then again, I can't say I'm surprised."

"Do I know you?" the man asked. He was big, unshaven, but Jeff would have recognized him anywhere.

"We've met, if only briefly, Herr Reinhart," Jeff said, sarcastically.

"You know my name?" Reinhart peered into Jeff's face. "You voice sounds familiar, but your appearance is not. I've had dealings with you people before, but I don't recall your face, and I never forget a face."

Jeff stripped off his garment. "No need to pretend anymore," he said.

"You're an American," Reinhart said. "Now I understand. We've been betrayed, but I still don't know who you are."

"Does the name *Chartrand* ring a bell, Herr Reinhart?"

The big man gave Jeff a closer look. "Ah, yes, now I recognize you. My *Indianer* friend with the French name. You didn't have a beard when we met."

"I am not an Indian and neither am I French. I am an American, remember that," Jeff spoke sharply, irritated by the man's familiar tone. "And I'm not your friend."

Reinhart chuckled. "Last time we drank *Schnapps* together." His German accent seemed to be much heavier than before.

Jeff sighed. "You're putting me into an awkward position, Reinhart. What am I supposed to do with you?"

"Let me have that jeep and I'll disappear. Pretend we never met." Reinhart grinned broadly.

"You know I can't do that." Jeff looked at the other prisoners. "You are all guilty of committing treason against the United States of America, a crime punishable by death!"

"Hold it now, sir," one of the prisoners spoke up. "You got this all wrong. We're only delivering weapons to a group of local militiamen. You, I mean the people who were supposed to get these weapons, are on our side. Apparently, they can't get weapons the official way, so we supply them unofficially."

"Who told you that crap?"

"The Serge did."

"The Serge? Really?" He looked at the dead man with the small mustache. "It seems he's dead, which means we can't ask him." He stared at the men. "Who else believed that?"

Most of the prisoners lifted their hands, but not all of them. Jeff made a mental note of the ones who didn't. Then he glared at Reinhart. "What is your version, Herr Reinhart?"

The big man shrugged. "I make no secret that I knew what this was all about. It was a business transaction."

Jeff laughed humorlessly. "Remind me never to deal with you or your friends." He pointed at the smoking rubble of the second house. "Lucky for you that house was empty, or I would have you all shot right here and now! That doesn't look like an honest business deal to me. Your employers were not quite truthful and, obviously, they don't give a shit about you."

His eyes fixed on Reinhart. "Aside from you, who else here knew what was going to happen to your business partners?"

Reinhart pointed out the four men who had not lifted their hands. The same men Jeff had already marked. He told them to step away from the others. "I want you to tell me who your employers are. Names and details of your operations."

One of the four laughed. "You can go and fuck yourself, whoever you are. You can't touch us. I know my rights. I demand you let us go immediately."

Jeff glared at him. The man was tall, wide shouldered, his face swarthy, his lips cruel. Jeff didn't like him. "You demand? What's your name, soldier?"

"George Stiller. Ex-marine. Lieutenant to you. That is all I'm going to tell you."

"Well, thank you, Lieutenant. Let me introduce myself. I am Lieutenant Jeffrey Chartrand and I'm the man who decides what rights you have. Actually, you don't have any!" Jeff said coldly. "You are a disgrace to the uniform you're wearing and you don't make demands!"

"My father is a lawyer." His lips turned up in a snarl.

"Good for your father but not so good for you. I hate lawyers." He signaled to Rob. "Take him away. You know what to do."

Rob put a gun to Stiller's head. "Let's go."

"Where are you taking me?"

"Shut up!" Rob told him, giving him a push. "Walk!"

Jeff stared in silence at the other three. They glared back at him, defiance in their faces and eyes.

When the single shot rang out from behind the shed, they all stared at him in horror, but they kept their mouths shut.

"Anyone else trying to impress me?" Jeff asked. He felt cold inside, knowing he had condemned a man to death in cold blood, but he felt no remorse.

"Can I speak to you in private, Lieutenant Chartrand?" Reinhart asked, a slight tremor in his voice.

"What about?"

"In private, please."

"All right." Jeff looked at Suliman. "Shoot anyone who makes a wrong move."

"Yes, sir, Lieutenant." He took the M-16 from Jeff, who didn't even bother to take his pistol from its holster as he walked away with Reinhart.

They stopped near the Jeep, within visible range of Jeff's men.

They'd be able to hear the conversation through Jeff's earpiece. "What is it you want, Reinhart?"

"I want to make a deal."

"I'm listening."

"Take me back to America, pay me one hundred thousand dollars and I'll tell you who I'm working for. I'll give you all the information you want to know."

"Tell me now and I will take you to a military prison in Baghdad. As soon as we have confirmed what you tell us is true we'll put you on a plane to your Fatherland Germany. No charge." Jeff smiled. "I'm afraid no hundred thousand dollars. That's the best I can do."

"No deal," Reinhart said. "I want to go to America. I feel safer there."

Jeff thought it over. "Okay, but you'd better deliver."

Reinhart smiled. "You won't be sorry, my friend."

"I'm not your friend, Reinhart," Jeff said coldly. "Remember that."

They walked back to the others.

"Search them for weapons and then put them into one of the sheds. Make sure they don't escape." He spoke to Armano and Hung. "You two guard them with your life." He turned away, looked for Rob. "Have you seen Kalila?"

Rob shrugged. "No. Last I saw her she was in the house."

"Kalila?" Jeff called.

When she didn't answer, his heart suddenly beat faster, and he hurried toward to the house, ripped open the door. Flicking on the light, he saw her lying on the floor. A dark stain discolored the rough boards under her.

Rushing to her, he knelt down beside her, touched her neck and breathed a sigh of relief when he detected a pulse. Blood covered one side of her face. "Springer, Harmon! On the double into the house!"

There was glass on the floor. When he looked at the window, he saw that it had been shattered.

Ripping open Kalila's garment, he undid her shirt to expose her upper body. Blood oozed out of a wound in her left shoulder.

Springer was the first one to enter.

"Get a med kit," Jeff told him, and then he looked at Harmon, who came rushing through the door. "We're leaving immediately. I want to

75

get Miss Ahmed to the hospital as quickly as possible. She's been shot."

Harmon stared at Kalila lifeless body. "How bad is it?"

Jeff shrugged. "I'm not a medic. One bullet hit her shoulder and another one her head. She's unconscious. That can't be a good sign. I can't tell how much damage either bullet did. Go prepare everyone for a quick departure."

Springer came back with a med kit and took out some gauze and disinfectant spray.

"How good are you with fixing up a patient?" Jeff asked.

"I remember enough from my first aid course."

"Then go ahead and see what you can do for her."

Springer lifted Kalila gently and put his hand under her shoulder. When he brought it back, it was full of blood. "The bullet went through her. There could be bone fragments. She may need to be operated on. All I can do is patch her up from both sides to stop the bleeding and prevent contamination."

Jeff helped him to pull away her clothing further and bare the back of her shoulder. Her garment and shirt were soaked with blood behind her shoulder blade.

She moaned and her eyelids fluttered open.

"Jeff?" she asked, trying to focus her eyes on his face.

"I'm here, Kalila," he said softly. Then he removed the transmitter from inside his ear and shoved it into his pocket. He did the same with hers. There was no need for the whole team to listen in.

She smiled and tried to lift her hand, winced and gave it up. "How bad is it?"

He shook his head. "I won't lie to you. It could be bad, I don't know. We'll have to get you to a doctor."

She opened her mouth to say something, and then she coughed and cried out. Jeff stared at the blood on her lips. "We'll give you something for the pain." He nodded to Springer, who removed a small plastic bag from his kit, ripped it open and fitted a needle to a syringe. Then he took Kalila's arm and injected the drug.

She relaxed and smiled bravely. Lifting her other arm, she put her hand against Jeff's cheek. "Take care of Omar, promise me."

"I promise." He choked back a sob. *Fuck it! When will this end?*

"You could come with me to the States and make sure I'll keep my promise." He put his hand on hers.

She shook her head. Her face seemed suddenly gray. "It would not work. You know that. You and I…we are from different worlds."

Jeff moved away when Springer pushed him gently aside. "Let me dress the wound, sir," he said with a low voice.

Jeff watched him spray the wound on her chest and then on her back. After that, he applied some gauze and taped it up, careful not to touch her exposed breast.

She's got lovely breasts. The thoughts popped into his head, unbidden and insane at a moment when she may be dying. The last thing he should be interested in right now was the shape of her breasts, but the mind does strange things to a man under duress.

Harmon came back in. "We're ready to move out, sir."

"What did you do with the prisoners?"

"We've put them onto one of the trucks."

"Good. Don't let any of them escape. If they try shoot them," Jeff said grimly. He was disgusted with all of them. Perhaps some were ignorant of the true situation and really thought they were doing a good thing. He didn't know.

Were you one of those guys who had no idea what you were involved in, Michael?

Kalila lay on the floor, looking up at him. Springer finished up and, gently, put her clothing back into place.

"Give Springer a hand with Miss Ahmed. Put her into the back of one of the trucks. Take all of the garments we wore and use them to make her comfortable. I'll be riding in the back with her."

He crouched down beside Kalila and touched her hand. "We'll get you to a hospital. Just hang on. I'll see you later." He rose and went outside, looking for Rob. When he found him, he told him to take the rocket launcher off the truck and make room for Kalila.

"What do you want us to do about the dead?" Rob asked.

"Dump them all into the house and then put a rocket into it. Let it all burn!"

"You want their dog tags?"

"No. Erase all evidence they ever existed." Jeff stalked away, his mind like ice and his thoughts full of hate. Remembering his earpiece, he put it back into his ear. He needed to stay in touch with the team.

Springer and Armano brought Kalila, carrying her in a temporary stretcher made from one of the white garments. They put her into the truck. Springer went and collected all of the garments and used them to make a bed for Kalila.

Jeff waited until Rob and Hung fired a missile into the house, watched it blow up like fireworks on the Fourth of July. Then he joined Kalila in the truck.

"Let's go," he told his men. The truck began rolling.

Chapter Nine

Baghdad was silhouetted against the eastern sky.

"It used to be a beautiful city." Colonel Settler looked out of the field hospital's window, sighed and turned back to Jeff. "What you ask is impossible," he said. "She is an Iraqi."

"She has an American passport."

Settler smiled, stroking his bushy mustache. "A forgery, you know that."

"A very good one. Made by an American government agency." Jeff felt frustrated. "If she doesn't get operated on, she'll die, Colonel. I can't let that happen and I don't believe you want that on your conscience."

Settler stared at Jeff. "Why do you care what happens to Lieutenant Ahmed? She's a Muslim and you're a Christian. You're on opposite sides of the fence. The Muslims hate us and our way of life." He gave Jeff a sharp look. "Is there something going on between you two, Lieutenant?"

Jeff cleared his throat, trying hard to find the right words to say it. "If you're asking have we slept together, the answer is no. Do I have feelings for her? Yes, I have, I'll make no secret about that, and you are correct, she and I, we have nothing in common except for that little boy we rescued. He is my dead brother's and her sister's son. I feel an obligation toward her."

"I understand, but that is purely personal, between you and her. It has nothing to do with American interests." The colonel's dark eyes rested on Jeff. "How can I justify the expense of sending an Iraqi woman to a hospital in Germany?"

"Pretend she's an American, Colonel. She has a passport to prove it. She saved Sergeant Abduk's and my life by leading us to safety on our first mission. Let's save her life now."

"I'll see what I can do." Colonel Settler walked away.

Jeff looked after him. He had come to like the short, heavyset man, who reminded him so much of his uncle Gerard Chartrand. He had sprouted a thick bushy mustache just like that, and even in his manners, Settler seemed so much like Uncle Gerard. Michael had not cared much for the somewhat eccentric uncle, and Jeff never understood why. Michael had always said he'd tell him some day, but that was another secret he took with him into his early grave.

Well, Michael, you should be happy now. Your son is safe. He'll be a member of the family, the only one to carry on the family name. He is safe but, unfortunately, I am not. I have to go back home to my country where I'm still wanted by the law for killing a man you had dealings with. Michael, oh, Michael. Even from the grave, you're still making me clean up your mess. This is not the first time, but this time it's serious.

He decided to go back into the room to speak to Kalila again. Most of the beds were occupied by soldiers who had been seriously wounded. He knew of at least two of them who would be airlifted to a hospital in Germany the next morning, where they would get the treatment they needed.

He hoped Kalila would join them.

She turned her head and smiled at him when he walked up to her. "I thought you left," she said. Her voice sounded slurred because of the medication.

He crouched beside her bed and looked into her eyes, which she desperately tried to keep open. "I spoke to Colonel Settler. He'll try to get you on a plane to Germany." He searched for her hand and touched it. "I won't abandon you, Kalila."

She pulled her lips into a little smile. They were cracked and without much color. "Why are you doing this, Jeff?"

"You know why. Don't pretend you don't."

"I know," she whispered, and then she closed her eyes.

He waited for a while, wanted her to say more, but she seemed to be fast asleep. He rose, bent over her and kissed her on the forehead. Then he walked away quickly, not looking at any of the other beds.

Outside, the sun burned mercilessly and the wind punished his exposed skin with hot particles of sharp sand.

I can't wait to leave this forsaken place. I don't know why we bother with it.

He hadn't seen the rest of the team, except for Rob, since they came back from the mission. These last two days passed so quickly with writing reports and filling out forms that explained the use of government property and the nature of the mission.

"It would have been better if there hadn't been any prisoners," Colonel Settler told him after they arrived back in the compound. "You and your men aren't even supposed to be here. There are no records. You are ghosts. You don't exist. Luckily, I sent Suliman with you. In addition, I've got a couple of loyal soldiers who will ask no questions if their names suddenly appear on a mission they know nothing about. By the way, what happened to the two million dollars counterfeit money you mentioned?"

"We burnt it."

"Good. The weapons you've brought will be put into inventory."

"What about the prisoners?"

"The enlisted men…I'll have them questioned and then I'll let them get back to their units. They can explain their absence to their CO. The mercenaries will be put into a military prison. I don't know how long we can hold them. And that German feller, Reinhart, he's your responsibility."

"Don't worry about Reinhart. I've made a deal with him and I'll honor it, if he keeps his part of the deal."

* * * *

Colonel Settler kept his word. He put Kalila on the plane to Germany the next morning. She would get the operation she needed in a proper hospital.

Jeff's plane left the day after and he was none too happy to leave *Hell* behind. "If I never see an Arabian country again, it will still be too soon," he told his men as they boarded the plane. He was glad to see everybody. Except for Sergeant Abduk, nobody had been wounded or, worse, killed.

Reinhart took the seat Abduk occupied on the flight from the US to Iraq. Jeff refrained from putting shackles on the big German. He was inside a military plane, thirty thousand feet in the air. There was no place to run.

Besides, he would not get far. Rob and his men would see to that. Had it not been for Jeff, Reinhart would be dead. None of them really cared much one way or the other if the company that built and sold weapons to insurgents was ever found.

It would not stop the illegal trading of arms. They had no such illusions.

"It's all political," Harmon commented when Jeff tried to explain why he needed Reinhart alive. "We close down one company and soon another one will take its place. It's like dealing with drug pushers. You can't eliminate them. All we can do is prevent the deals from taking place. We've done that. That's good enough for me."

Jeff closed his eyes and tried to get some sleep. It felt good to be back on American soil, even if they were in the air and still thousands of miles away from the homeland. This was American property. Even the air inside the plane smelled good.

* * * *

Colonel Cowley did not meet the team members after the bus dropped them off in the military base; instead, a tall, gaunt man, who identified himself as Colonel O'Connor, waited for them.

"Colonel Cowley has been relieved of his post and I am the new head of his department," he told them. His eyes locked with Jeff's. "You must be Lieutenant Chartrand."

Jeff returned his stare, feeling an instant dislike for the man. "If you say so then I must be him, sir." He didn't care for the man and neither did he care for the two heavily armed marines with him.

O'Connor scowled. "I would like to have a word with you, Lieutenant."

"Can it wait, sir? I wouldn't mind heaving a shower and a change of clothing first. We've had a long flight."

"No, it can't wait. You'll accompany me now!" He glared at the others. "None of you leave the base until you've been debriefed."

"What about me?" Reinhart asked.

O'Connor gave him a sharp look. "Who are you?"

Reinhart smiled disarmingly. "My name is Werner Reinhart. These fine gentlemen have been so kind to rescue me in Iraq from certain death and allowed me to come with them to your fine country. I appreciate it very much, but I guess I'll be going now."

"What do you mean they allowed you to come to our country?" The colonel's gaze shifted to Jeff. "Explain the presence of this man! Is he even an American?"

"He is a German and he is our prisoner, sir. I've made a deal with him."

"What kind of a deal?"

"His freedom in exchange for information."

"I know nothing about this!" O'Connor eyed Jeff with suspicion. "I want both of you in my office."

Jeff grimaced at Reinhart. "You heard the Colonel, Reinhart. I guess your departure will have to wait a little while longer."

The big German shrugged. "I am not in much of a hurry."

Colonel O'Connor took them into his office. It wasn't Cowley's office, of that Jeff was certain, because he didn't see anything that would indicate that Colonel Cowley had ever been here.

O'Connor sank into a leather chair behind a massive desk. He didn't offer Jeff or Reinhart a seat. The two marines took their positions near the door.

"What's this about, Colonel?" Jeff asked.

"I'll be asking the questions, Lieutenant, if you don't mind."

"Then ask, sir."

O'Connor stared at him. "Lieutenant Chartrand, I haven't decided yet what to do about you. Your arrogant attitude might just sway my decision, and believe me it won't be in your favor." His gaze took in Reinhart. "Who is this man and what is this deal you've mentioned?"

"We caught him in Iraq trying to sell arms to terrorists. He works for an American arms dealer. I promised him his freedom if he supplies us with information that will lead us to the people he works for." Jeff looked at Reinhart. "Now would be a good time to enlighten us, Herr Reinhart."

The German sighed. "I might as well come clean now. I don't know who sells these weapons. I'm only a delivery boy and I was hired by a private employment agency from Dallas. That's all I know. I'm not really interested who I work for, as long as my money gets deposited to my account."

"You must be kidding, Reinhart!" Jeff spoke hotly. "You let me believe you knew who the sellers are."

"Sorry, if I misled you, Chartrand." Reinhart lifted his beefy shoulders and spread his hands. "I had to do something to save my life. I mean, the way you dealt with that Lieutenant, that was cold."

"I'm getting the impression you screwed up, Lieutenant." O'Connor didn't hide his satisfaction.

"That may be so, Colonel, but at least we'll know who hired him. We can take it from there."

"We'll see. It may not be in our best interest to pursue that road. We are not a private detective agency. This is the Military, don't forget that, Lieutenant. Our goals are not the same as the goals of civilians."

"I work for Military Intelligence, sir. It is my job to find the enemy, sir. Anyone selling arms to terrorists is considered *The Enemy*," Jeff said sharply.

"Do not speak to me in that tone, Lieutenant Chartrand!" O'Connor gestured to the marines. "Take the civilian and put him into a secure room. Then station yourselves outside my office. I want to talk to the Lieutenant in private."

"Yes, sir." They grabbed the German's arms and took him outside.

O'Connor's blue eyes looked coldly at Jeff. "You said you work for Military Intelligence, Lieutenant? There is no record of this in my files. You were discharged from the army 1991 after being wounded in action. Tell me, what are you doing here?"

It was Jeff's turn to stare at the colonel, a feeling of impending doom settling in his stomach. "Didn't Colonel Cowley fill you in, sir?"

"About what?"

"Our mission. About me?"

"Colonel Cowley's record keeping is at best very sketchy. To put it plain and simple...there are no records. None that I can find. His conduct in the Military has come under scrutiny, and so has his unit. Colonel Cowley is being investigated for possibly being involved in criminal activities." O'Connor leaned forward. "We've intercepted a message from a Colonel Settler, who is stationed in Baghdad. That's how we found out about your presence there. What exactly did you do in Iraq?"

"That is classified information. You'll have to ask Colonel Cowley, sir."

"I'm asking you."

"Begging your pardon, sir. I have only your word that you have replaced Colonel Cowley. I will report only to him."

O'Connor rose in his seat and pointed a finger at Jeff. "You are testing my patience, Chartrand! As far as I know, you are a civilian and a fugitive from the law, hiding in a military compound for reasons unknown. Homeland Security has put you on the watch list. You weren't even supposed to leave the country, yet, here you are, just returned from Iraq."

"Like I said, talk to Colonel Cowley." Jeff was determined not to let O'Connor intimidate him. He was suspicious of the man, since he didn't know him. Who's to say he was really the man he claimed to be?

"To my knowledge you have no status in the Military except as an ex-marine. I looked into your old records and what do you suppose I found?" O'Connor's eyes practically speared Jeff.

"I don't know, sir." Jeff shrugged, waiting patiently for the colonel to tell him, as he knew he would.

"You were part of Cowley's unit back then, known as 'The Corporation'. Even then, he kept lousy records."

"May I remind you that I was in Military Intelligence, sir," Jeff said. "Some of our operations naturally dictated a certain...umm...stealth and omission of information."

"Are you telling me you were involved in illegal activities?"

"I'm not saying that at all. I'm saying some investigations required us to work in secret if we were to be successful." Jeff allowed himself a conspiratorial smile. "Most of our missions were top secret. Still are. You know how that is, Colonel. You are in the Intelligence Service."

"What makes you assume that?"

"Well, you said that you are the new head of Colonel Cowley's department. That would be the Intelligence Branch. Is that not correct?"

"It is correct."

"Then, sir, you know everything about the Grey Ops?"

"I know nothing about the Grey Ops and its operations. Only Colonel Cowley and the men in his unit know. There are no records anywhere. Until now, Grey Ops was a ghost unit. It didn't exist. Not officially."

O'Connor sighed. His eyes lost their icy stare and became calculating. "I'm giving you a chance here, Chartrand. Tell me about some of the operations you were involved in twenty years ago and about this latest one. Give me locations and names of the soldiers involved and I will try my best to make all of your charges go away."

"And if I don't?"

"I will hand you over to Homeland Security. In chains."

Jeff tried to think fast, looking for a way out. "You're asking a lot, Colonel. It's been twenty years. I was wounded in the Gulf war. Things are a little fuzzy. I tried to forget."

"Are you refusing my request?"

"No, I'm not, but you have to give me time to think about it. I'll have to write things down, let them jog my memory. Also, I wouldn't mind cleaning up first."

"Twenty-four hours. That's all you've got!"

"Thank you, Colonel. One more request."

"What is it?" O'Connor sounded irritated, impatient to get this over with.

Jeff smiled, somewhat embarrassed. "I'm not familiar with the base. Where are the showers and where can I bunk?"

O'Connor shook his head, clearly annoyed. "I'll have someone direct you. Now, go and wait in the hall outside."

Jeff saluted, grabbed his duffel bag and stepped out of the office. He gave the two marines in front of the door a friendly smile. "I'm supposed to wait for someone," he told them.

They didn't smile back, just watched him as he stood on the other side, leaning against the wall.

Fuck it! There seems to be no end to my misfortune. How the hell can I get myself out of this one?

Chapter Ten

Feeling much better after his shower, Jeff went in search of the mess hall. It was close to suppertime, and when he found it, there were a number of soldiers lining up for their food. He spotted Rob and the others already sitting at a table.

He joined them after getting a tray and sat down across from Rob. "It seems we have a problem," he told them. "It involves you also."

"What did Colonel O'Connor want?" Rob asked.

"I think he's on a witch hunt. What the hell happened while we were gone? Do you know this colonel?"

"I do." Rob nodded. "He's Army Intelligence, but from a different branch. Something like Internal Affairs. He's also a Politician and has his sights set on a seat in the Senate. His aim is to expose corruption in the Military. Wants to clean it up."

"I don't trust him, Rob." Jeff felt a weight in his belly and he knew it had nothing to do with the food he was consuming. "He gave me an ultimatum. Either give him details about Grey Ops missions or he'll throw me to the wolves, namely Homeland Security."

Rob tilted his head, his eyes grave as he studied Jeff. "How long do you have?"

"Twenty-four hours."

"He's had it out for my father for a long time and it looks as if he's finally made his move. We'll have to get you out of here, you know that, Lieutenant."

"I know, but how?"

Rob smiled. "You're part of the team now, sir. We won't abandon you."

They finished eating in silence as other soldiers joined them at their table.

"I need to talk to Reinhart," Jeff said, before they parted. "He claims he doesn't know anything, but I need to know who hired him."

"I'll find out, sir. I have friends on this base."

Jeff's roommates were mostly new recruits, eager to get to Iraq. He felt sorry for them. They didn't know what they were facing. What he had seen in Iraq left him convinced more than ever that this war was turning out to be another Vietnam. He remembered Samantha's brother Frank Bailey, the attorney, talking to him at the funeral.

It will be a long time before there is peace in the region. If ever.

Jeff argued with him at the time, but now he was ready to agree. How many Americans had to die until the Sunnis and Shi'a began building up their country instead of fighting each other over whose religion was the right one? When would they stop the terrorist attacks? When would there be an end to young men blowing themselves up for a cause that made no logical sense to a rational person?

He thought about Kalila and wondered how she was doing. She believed in her country, and her people. If only there were more like her.

When he finally fell asleep, he dreamed about Connie and Maxine. They accused him of cheating on them with Kalila and he woke wishing something had actually happened between Kalila and him. He missed her more than he had ever missed anyone.

Rob met him again in the mess hall. This time he was alone.

"I have the information you wanted from that German feller. He really doesn't know anything but the name of the company who hired him."

"How did you manage to get the information?"

Rob shrugged, smiling like someone who just finished eating a sour apple. "I had no trouble finding him. They're holding him in a room guarded by one of the recruits. I guess they don't really care if he escapes or not. He's a charmer, that German, and I don't believe he'll be here much longer. They'll let him go. I had to lean on him a bit, before he quite reluctantly gave away his little secret."

He grinned a little. "Did you promise him money, sir?"

"I promised him his freedom, nothing else." Jeff wondered what Rob meant when he said he leaned on Reinhart. He didn't think the big German was easily intimidated.

"We'll move shortly after lunch, sir." Rob spoke in a low voice. "I see you haven't shaved off your beard, yet. That's good. We'll have to trim it a little and I was thinking red would be a nice touch."

"What?" Jeff had only been listening with one ear to what Rob was saying, thinking about Reinhart and his gentlemanly manners.

"I said red would be a nice touch."

"For what?"

"Your hair and your beard." Rob gave him his innocent little boy's grin. "I think you'd look quite sophisticated. Like a professor or maybe a Chiropractor."

"Why a Chiropractor?"

"I went to one once who looked like that." Rob sounded suddenly enthusiastic. "That's what we'll do. Your new identity will be a Chiropractor."

Jeff shook his head. "Hold it, young man. I'm not following you here. Why would I want to be a Chiropractor?"

"After your escape from here, Colonel O'Connor will be furious and will want your hide. On top of that, Homeland Security will be after you again." He became serious. "I realize, changing your appearance and giving you a false passport will only be a temporary measure, but it will be adequate for a while. We can't change your fingerprints; you'll have to keep a low profile until we can prove that you are no threat to national security. That other problem you have, well, I don't know if we can help you with that."

"I'll deal with that when I have to. Our most important task is to expose the company or companies who sell arms to terrorists. They are the real enemies of our country," Jeff said.

Rob looked thoughtful. "That may be so, but the people who own those companies are business people. They see an opportunity to make a buck and they're taking advantage of it. Would you call the oil companies *Enemies of the State?*"

"Not the State but enemies of the people. Look at gas prices. We're being ripped off."

Rob smiled. "I'm not talking about gas prices, but I know what you mean. No, I'm talking about the real reason we invaded Iraq. Oil. Iraq is the riches oil country in the world. American oil companies want to control the supply of oil. That's why we are still in Iraq."

It surprised Jeff to hear Rob talking like that. "I had no idea you felt that way, Rob. I would be careful about making my views known to certain people, my young friend. Especially those families who have lost loved-ones over there. Does your father, Colonel Cowley, share your radical views?"

"These are my views, not his. We don't discuss politics. I'm not alone in this. Many people agree with me. You were in Iraq. You saw the people there. They hate us and they want us out. Our politicians know this fact, as does our president. You know why he can't pull our troops out of Iraq? Because he is an oilman and he is controlled by other oilmen. That's why."

"Wow, Rob! You must have given this a lot of thought. I never knew you were this cynical. Answer me one question. Why are you fighting in this war if you feel the way you do?"

"Because I am a soldier and a patriot. I have sworn allegiance to the American Flag. I will fight for my country, even if it is for the wrong cause."

"You are a true loyalist, Rob," Jeff said, "but I'm not sure if that is such a good thing."

Rob finished his breakfast and rose. "Be ready to move after lunch, sir. I'll see you then."

* * * *

They were all there at dinnertime.

Rob, Armano, Springer, Harmon, and Hung.

Harmon reached across the table and shook Jeff's hand. "Good luck, sir. I hope you can clear your name."

The other men nodded gravely. "It's a bummer." Springer spoke softly. "It was an honor to serve under you, sir. You're all right."

"Thank you. I hope you guys won't be affected by Colonel O'Connor's investigation."

Rob grinned. "He has nothing on us. My father is a careful man. We were never in Iraq. This mission never took place."

"What about the records you kept?"

"What records, sir?" He gave Jeff his innocent grin. "There are no records. I was writing a novel."

Jeff's laughter made other soldiers turn their heads and he let it end in a chuckle. "You do not stop to surprise me, young man. I didn't know you were a writer. What are you writing?"

"A mystery thriller. About a man, a soldier, falsely accused of a crime and his efforts to clear his name."

"Sounds interesting, but it is nothing new."

"Most murder mysteries carry the same theme. The secret is to add a twist that makes it new." Rob gave a sigh. "And that is the part that provides the greatest challenge for me. It is not easy to come up with something that hasn't been done before."

"Well, I wish you success. I have no doubt you will achieve it. You are a remarkable young man." Jeff looked at the others. "All of you are. I am honored to have made your acquaintance."

Hung, who was usually the quiet one, gave a low chuckle. "Don't dismiss us yet, Lieutenant. We'll be coming with you when you leave."

"I was under the impression you were told to stay on the base."

"I pulled a few strings and I made some inquiries," Rob said. "As I told you, I have many friends here, and so has my father. Colonel O'Connor has no authority over us."

"Where is Colonel Cowley?"

"Probably at his country home planting a rosebush. He always wanted to do that." Rob laughed. "Don't worry about him. He's a tough old bird. Guys like O'Connor will never measure up to him. He eats them for breakfast. Don't you think he's made contingency plans for situations like this one?"

"I'm sure he has. He is a careful and clever man," Jeff said, agreeing with Rob's statement."

"We should leave before O'Connor's marines come looking for you, Lieutenant." Rob looked appreciatively at Jeff's duffle bag. "I see you came prepared."

"So have you, I notice," Jeff said.

"I couldn't very well let you go all by yourself." Rob shouldered his own bag. "I've put in for a couple of weeks of furlough. I deserve it."

Outside the mess hall, one of the military trucks pulled up and they all piled into the back, Jeff included. "One of my buddies is driving," Rob explained. "The guard at the gate is also a good friend of mine. He won't look too closely."

The truck stopped for only a short moment by the guardhouse and then it started rolling again. When it finally came to a halt for a second time, Rob said, "We'll get off here."

Jeff said goodbye to the other men, who had come along only as a diversion, and then he jumped onto the street. When he looked around, he recognized the warehouse where he had been hiding out.

"We'll be safe here until tomorrow. Then we'll move on," Rob explained. "Everything we need is here."

It was evident nobody used the suite during the time they were in Iraq. The cell phone, Morgan gave him to be used only in an emergency, still lay on the counter where Jeff left it.

Rob used it to make a call. Then he said, "Now let's get you ready for your new persona." He went into the bedroom Kalila used and brought back a barber kit.

"First, I'm going to shape your beard and cut your hair and then we'll color it."

Jeff had to shake his head again. "Is there anything you can't do?" he asked.

"You'd be surprised." Rob smiled. "I've never been able to compose a song."

"Well, thank goodness for that." Jeff chuckled. "I don't think I could stand it if you composed a song while cutting my hair."

"You don't have to worry about that, sir." Rob proceeded cutting Jeff's hair and to trim his beard. When it was done to his satisfaction, he applied the hair color. "Well, I think you'll like yourself," Rob said. "The color suits you."

Jeff inspected Rob's handiwork and had to admit that it didn't look bad, but he wasn't quite sure if he liked the carrot red color. "I think it draws attention to my person."

"To the contrary, sir. Everybody will concentrate on the red color but will forget to look closer at your face. I think it's perfect." He studied Jeff from all sides. "It gives you that sophisticated look."

About an hour later, someone knocked on the door. Rob opened it to let in a short, chubby man. He high-fived Rob and then he looked at Jeff. "Hi, there. I'm Billy, the guy who will give you a new identity."

"Hi, Billy," Jeff said. "I'm Jeff."

Billy shook his head. "Not anymore. You are Dr. Richard Callwell."

"Doctor?" Jeff lifted an eyebrow and looked at Rob.

Rob nodded, smiling. "Dr. Richard Raymond Callwell. Chiropractor."

Billy produced a passport and handed it to Jeff. "All we need is your picture to make it legal."

Jeff opened the passport and studied it. "It says here I'm a Canadian, living in Toronto." He gave Billy a questioning look. "Canadian?"

Billy shrugged and pointed at Rob. "His idea."

"You've taken time off from a stressful job. That way nobody will ask you to fix their back or whatever ails them. You're not allowed to work in the States."

"Very clever. What about this address in Toronto?"

"Legitimate," Billy said. "I have an old aunt who lives there. Her last name is Callwell."

"What if anyone questions her?"

Billy waved it off. "Don't worry about that. She's a bit senile, can't remember things too well. My cousin died a number of years ago. His name was Richard. She hasn't accepted it to this day. Thinks he's still alive, just left for greener pastures."

He went over to the large bag he brought with him and produced a digital camera. "Okay, look into the camera and don't smile. Can't smile on a passport picture."

When he was done, he stashed away his camera. "All I need is your signature and then I'll be on my way. I'll have it back by tomorrow morning."

"Tonight," Rob said, gently.

"Can't do. As it is, I dropped everything just for this."

Rob chuckled. "You'll deliver it tonight or I'll feed you your balls for breakfast, Billy."

"All right, all right, but you owe me a favor."

"It'll be a long time until I owe you any favors, my little *Chubby One*." Rob spoke softly, but Jeff didn't miss the underlying threat in his words. He wondered what Rob held over Billy.

After Billy left, Jeff asked, "Who is he?"

"A smalltime hood and a brilliant counterfeiter. We've tried to recruit him, but he prefers to stay independent."

"You trust him?"

"As far as I can spit."

"That far?" Jeff had to laugh the way Rob said it.

"However, I wouldn't worry about him. He will never betray me."

"How do you know?"

"Because he's my cousin. You know what they say…blood is thicker than water."

"Your cousin?" Jeff shook his head, puzzled. "Does that mean this Mrs. Callwell in Toronto is your aunt, also?"

"You got it, oh Wise One." Rob grinned hugely, greatly amused by something. "That makes you my cousin from Canada. Small world isn't it. Amazing how some things just seem to fall into place."

"You've got a strange sense of humor, Rob."

Billy came back later that night with the completed passport. He even brought a driver's license.

"I don't think I'll need that," Jeff said.

Billy shrugged. "I thought it was a nice touch. You never know, it might come in handy some day. I'm throwing it in as a bonus."

Chapter Eleven

"I suppose I don't have a bank account in my name?"

"Sorry. There are limits to what I can do."

"Then tell me, what are we going to do for money? I'm flat broke and unable to work, since you made me a Canadian. In addition, I couldn't, even if I had a chance to make some extra money. I know nothing about chiropractic."

"You won't need any money," Rob explained. "I'll look after that part. I have a credit card on an account monitored by Elias Morgan. Remember him? The lawyer who sprung you from the cops?"

"Of course I do. How can I forget him? Captain Elias Morgan, who knows everything about me. Another man who could sign my entry into state prison."

"He knows he needs to keep his mouth shut because he would also implicate himself. We are all in this together. Anyway, he pays all the bills."

Jeff was leery about taking a plane. The heightened security checks only increased the risk of being discovered, but he needn't have worried. The flight attendant barely glanced at his new passport when they boarded the plane. "Enjoy the flight," she said, flashing him an empty and bored smile.

The plane lifted off and Jeff heaved a sigh of relief.

"Well, Richard, my cousin," Rob said as he adjusted his seat. "Feel like having a drink?"

"I think I do. Order me a Scotch. Second thought, make it a double."

He tried to relax but found he was still jittery. Being a fugitive was not something he ever dreamed of becoming. He hated this whole situation. Playing second fiddle was not the way he liked to live. He needed to be in charge, needed to make the decisions. His whole life had always been like that.

"I hope the information the German gave us doesn't lead us down a false trail," Rob broke into his thoughts.

"Didn't you tell me you beat it out of him?" He looked up at the flight attendant and accepted his drink. Holding it under his nose, he inhaled the strong aroma. He was not really a connoisseur, wasn't actually fond of hard liqueur, but sometimes he appreciated a stiff drink.

This was one of those occasions.

Letting it trickle down his throat, he remembered the *Schnapps* he shared with Reinhart. He seemed like such a jovial fellow, but something in his manners roused Jeff's suspicions and he had not been wrong about the German.

He looked over at Rob, who seemed to be studying his drink. "Men like Reinhart are not honorable, not loyal, not even to their own country. People who can be bought are not trustworthy. I hate his kind. You should have let me put him out of his misery."

"You know better than to talk like that, Rob. I'm not a cold-blooded murderer, and it would have been murder." Even though Jeff had lowered his voice, he was leery discussing it in public. You never knew who might be listening. Directional microphones were cheap and readily available. As were all sorts of electronic devices.

"Not murder," Rob said. "An execution."

* * * *

It was late in the afternoon when they arrived in Dallas. They took a taxi downtown and rented two rooms in a hotel.

"Not the swankiest place," Jeff remarked when they sat in the dining room and had supper.

"No, it isn't," Rob agreed, "but the safest place to be, believe it or not. Fancy hotels attract too much attention."

After supper, Rob suggested they visit the bar, but Jeff declined. "I'm quite tired, Rob. Probably suffering from jet lag. I think I'll go to bed early."

Rob shrugged. "I always forget, you're an old man," but then he smiled. "No offense, sir. I just figured some female company might do both of us good. It's been a while for me." He grinned. "And I'm still a young buck, aching to be held prisoner in the passionate embrace of a woman."

"I forgive you, young buck." Jeff slapped him on the back. "You go and have fun. Should you get lucky, I don't need to know in the morning. Okay?"

"Don't worry. I'm not in the habit of telling. You might remember I was trained to keep secrets." Rob laughed and headed for the bar.

Jeff's eyes followed him. Then he turned and took the elevator up to his room.

I'm also aching for the embrace of a beautiful, passionate woman, Rob, but not some stranger who might have screwed who knows how many other lonely men before me.

He was tempted to call Maxine and Connie, just to hear their voices and tell them he was all right, but he resisted that urge. It was too risky. Their phones could be tapped, or Maxine might try to talk him into giving himself up and take his chances in court. Something he was not willing to do.

Lying on his bed, he stared at the ceiling, thinking of Kalila. *Beautiful Kalila. I hope your operation was successful and you are recovering. Maybe some day we'll meet again.*

So much had happened these last few months. He found it hard to believe that over three months had passed since Michael's murder.

Monday, March 19, 2007.

That day would stay with him as long as he lived.

Funny, how there are certain things most people never forget.

The first love, the first kiss. The first sexual encounter. The first car. The death of a loved one.

It is amazing how many things there are, he thought. There are two more days I won't be able to forget, no matter how hard I try. January 29, 1991, when I was wounded in Kuwait, and February 27, 1997, the day I lost Nicole. I thought my life was over then. I would never love again, and here I am, ten years later, in love with not one but three women. Each one so different from the other two.

When he awoke and checked his watch, he saw that it was only a couple of minutes past six in the morning. He rose and took a shower, enjoying a luxury most Americans take for granted.

It would do every American some good to spend a few days in places like Iraq or Bosnia without running water, indoor toilets, air-conditioning. All the kids these days with their iPods, cell phones, videogames and other electronic gadgets, they have no idea how people in other countries live.

He dried himself off, looked at his image in the mirror and grinned. *I think Rob is right. I do look sophisticated with this beard. Maybe I'll keep it.*

Rob knocked on his door the moment he finished zipping up his pants.

"You must have been watching me on one of your spy devices," he said when he opened the door.

Rob tilted his head the way he sometimes did when he questioned something. "Why do you say that?"

"Never mind. Come on in. I'm surprised to see you this early. I would have thought you'd be exhausted after last night, unless…?" He didn't finish the sentence.

With a sly grin, Rob entered Jeff's room. "A gentleman enjoys and doesn't tell," he said. "Just to satisfy your curiosity, I did connect with a rather pretty, young lady. That's all I'm going to say. Use your imagination."

"You've already told me too much, blabbermouth." Jeff laughed. "Don't think I'm too old to imagine the rest."

Rob looked at Jeff with a critical eye. "You're looking good. Too bad you decided against joining me at the bar. The young lady's girlfriend was a little older but a knockout. You would have liked her. She was a redhead, like you."

"I'm not a redhead, Rob. You made me into one. So…what happened to that knockout?"

Rob shrugged. "I felt sorry for her, and I invited her into joining us in my room."

"Sounds interesting," Jeff said, "but again way too much information. I'm not really interested in your sexual escapades."

"You might be interested in the fact that this lady actually works for a recruiting agency."

Jeff gave Rob a sharp look. "Now that is interesting. Also strangely coincidental."

"Not really, considering that I'm a strapping young man and good material for adventure and great opportunities. Anyway, that's what she told me."

"Was she the one who approached you?"

"No." Rob shook his head. "My newly found young flame introduced us after I told her I might be looking for a job in Dallas. One never knows where dropping such information may lead."

"Would she possibly be working for the same agency we are looking for?"

"The very same. Again, not mysterious, because it is not far from here. She told me, she'd try to get us in today. They're not open for business Saturdays, but she's sure her boss will make an exception."

Jeff laughed. "Does her boss know what she's doing on the side?"

"It's probably a requirement of her job, working the nightclubs looking for recruits." Rob searched in his coat pocket and produced a business card. "Here. I'm supposed to phone this number at around ten o'clock. That's when her boss will be in the office."

"That is some stroke of luck," Jeff mused. "Maybe it is better than mentioning my good old friend Reinhart."

"It may not hurt to mention him also. Every little bit helps." Rob looked at Jeff. "Why don't we just go there and lean on these guys instead of going through this whole charade of pretending to join their outfit?"

"We can do that if all else fails, but I believe we'll get more information if we are part of the group. People tend to clam up if you put too much pressure on them."

"Well, we'll see." Rob didn't sound convinced. "How about going for breakfast?"

"Sounds good to me."

Rob made his call at exactly ten o'clock. "He said to come down," he told Jeff. We can walk. It's not far from here."

It took them twenty minutes to get to the place. The recruiting office was in an old rundown building, beside a Laundromat. Jeff studied the sign above the door for a moment.

PRIVATE GUARDS AND PROTECTION AGENCY.

Nothing to indicate whom they represented.

Shrugging, he opened the door and walked in. Rob followed close behind.

Nobody sat behind the front desk, and the waiting room was empty. A door at the end of the room stood open. Whoever was in there, must have heard them, because Jeff heard footsteps, and then a man in a uniform stepped out.

When he saw them, he smiled and held out a hand, looking at Jeff. "Are you Robert Cameron?"

Jeff hesitated for a moment and then he said, "No, I'm Richard Callwell. My partner here is Robert Cameron." He glanced at Rob. *It would have been helpful to know what name he was going to use.*

"Well, come on in. Before we can sign you up we'll have to take care of a few formalities." He sat down behind a large desk and smiled at them. "We're a bit understaffed today, since it's Saturday. My secretary has the day off." He winked at Rob. "I understand you've met one of our recruiting agents?"

"Yes, I have." Rob smiled back at him. "She was quite helpful."

"I'm sure she was. Miss Thomas is quite…umm…talented and dedicated to her job. She can be persuasive."

"I can certainly vouch for that. Very persuasive," Rob agreed.

"Oh, I'm sorry, I didn't introduce myself. I'm Mike Black, the owner of this agency." He studied the screen of his monitor. "I don't know if you've been informed about the kind of jobs we offer."

"According to the sign above your door, you provide jobs as private guards," Jeff ventured.

"That is correct, but we offer many other opportunities."

"Like what?"

"I'd like to find out a little more about you before we can decide what kind of job you might be suited for." He looked at Rob. "I might as well start with you. Have you ever fired a gun?"

Rob chuckled. "Yes, I have."

"Good. Have you ever been in the army?"

"Yes, I have."

"You're a soldier then. Very good. Been anywhere outside the United States?"

"In Iraq."

That brought a smile to Black's face. "Great. That opens up many opportunities for you. Are you currently employed?"

"No. That's why I'm here."

"Okay. I have some forms to fill out. Why don't you do that while I interview Mr. Callwell?" He shoved some papers across the desk and then he turned to Jeff.

"Ever fired a gun?"

"Sure. I'm a hunter and I belong to a gun club." Jeff took out his false passport. "Here, have a look at this. It might save some time."

Black took the passport, flicked it open and studied it for a moment. "You're a Canadian?"

"Yes, I am."

"What are you doing for a living?"

"I'm a Chiropractor."

"A Chiropractor? Hmm. Have you ever spent any time in the Canadian Armed Forces?"

"I'm a reservist." Jeff smiled. "On standby. I wouldn't mind seeing some action."

"Your people are in Afghanistan. Plenty of action there. Why not volunteer to go there?"

Jeff shrugged. "Actually, I'm considered too old. They want younger men. Besides, they don't pay much."

Black stared at Jeff. "If it's the money, why not stick to your occupation? I understand Chiropractors make a lot of money. More than doctors."

"I'm getting tired of cracking people's bones day after day. I'm itching for a change."

"Well, then you've come to the right place." He handed Jeff his passport and a few sheets of paper. "Fill them out and we'll take it from there. One more thing. Have you already applied for a work permit in the States?"

"No, I haven't."

"Would you be interested in working overseas? That pays well."

Jeff gave him a little smile. "Funny, you should mention that. I was in Germany a couple of months ago and spoke to a man by the name of Werner Reinhart. He told me about some great opportunities for making a lot of money. In fact, he's the man who put that bug in my ear and he also gave me your name. That is the reason why I came to Dallas in the first place."

"Really? That is quite interesting. Werner Reinhart. The name sounds familiar." His fingers danced over his keyboard. "You are right. He's actually in Iraq right now. I'm glad you mentioned him. References like that always speed up the hiring process."

The phone rang. "Excuse me." He picked up the receiver.

Jeff took the opportunity to look over the forms. He began filling them out and didn't pay much attention to Black's phone conversation. When he heard the click of the receiver being put in its place, he looked up to see Black regarding him silently. Something in his gaze disturbed Jeff. "Problem?"

Black smiled. Then he lifted a hand. "Can you give me a moment?"

"Sure. I'll just finish filling out these forms." Jeff looked at Rob. "How are you doing?"

"Just about finished," Rob said.

"Did you notice his change in attitude?" Jeff asked after Black disappeared through a door in the back.

"I wasn't watching him," Rob said. "They sure go into details on the third page of these forms."

Jeff chuckled. "You're the writer. Should be no problem for you to make up a few interesting stories about your life."

The opening of the door made him look up. Black stood within the doorframe, a gun in hand. A man in a black uniform, who also held a gun, accompanied him.

"What's going on?" Jeff asked.

"You tell me, Mr. Callwell. Or should I call you Mr. Chartrand?"

"You must have me confused with someone else," Jeff said, trying to bluff.

"I don't think so. You know who that was on the phone?"

Jeff shook his head. "No idea."

"Strange coincidence, really." Black grimaced. "That was Werner Reinhart. He told me a few interesting things. Disturbing things, actually. I may not have recognized you, with your red beard and hair, but your young friend over there was described to me in detail. Mr. Reinhart is a very good observer."

Jeff put down his pen and looked at Rob. "I think you were right. I should have let you take care of our friend Reinhart."

"You two had better leave before I call the cops," Black said with a cold voice.

"And tell them what? That we applied for a job? I don't believe that is a crime."

"Possession of a false passport and assuming another name is a crime." Black stepped into the room and waved with his gun. "You're lucky I don't just shoot you and say you tried to rob me."

Jeff laughed. "You are the guy with the gun. We have no weapons with us." He watched as the second man walked past Black and pointed his gun at Rob.

"Hey, Old-timer, watch where you point that gun. Someone could get hurt," Rob said.

"Get out! Both of you!" Black waved his gun again and came up to Jeff.

Rob stood up slowly, and then, with a quick movement, he disarmed the man who threatened him.

Jeff acted at the same instant. Black's attention had wavered and shifted to Rob. By the time Jeff moved in, it was too late for Black to defend himself successfully. Gripping the gun hand and pushing it aside, Jeff smashed his fist into Black's face, hitting him on the chin.

Black's eyes rolled up in their sockets. Then his body folded onto the floor like an old mattress.

Rob pinned his opponent to the floor and threatened him with his own gun.

"Please, don't shoot me, man! I'm just doing my job. Okay?" the man pleaded. His voice sounded muffled and strained.

Rob eased up and stepped back. "Get up! Slowly."

The man got up and brushed off his black uniform. "Who the fuck are you guys?"

Rob smiled. "We're the good guys, believe it or not."

"Are you cops?"

"In a way we are." Rob stared at him. "What's your name?"

"Jerry Mason."

"Are you working for this outfit, Jerry?"

"Only on weekends." He wiped his sleeve across his forehead.

Jeff noticed that the man was sweating profusely and his hands were shaking. He also noticed that he was quite old. Probably in his sixties.

"I'm doing this only to make some extra money. I'm actually a mechanic by trade."

"Maybe you should stick to fixing cars, Jerry," Rob said, chuckling. "You're too old for this kind of work. Now, sit in that chair over there and don't move, unless you want to get hurt." He smiled good-humoredly. "Take my advice, Jerry. Don't put on a uniform unless you can back it up."

Jeff turned his attention back to the man on the ground. Emitting a loud moan, Black began to stir. Then he opened his eyes, sat up and held his chin. Looking up at Jeff, he said, "You've got quite a punch. I could use a couple of guys like you in my outfit."

"I'm afraid we're on opposite sides," Rob growled. "We hunt and eliminate the guys who work for you."

"So I've heard. You've got one thing wrong, though. I'm only an employment agency, just a middleman. I provide the jobs, but I have nothing to do with the type of business the people who hire me are mixed up in."

"You are supplying mercenaries to people who are involved in the illegal arms trade, Mr. Black," Jeff said. "In the eyes of the law that makes you an accomplice."

Black held up both hands in a defensive gesture. "Hold it now. I know nothing about that. I get requests for a certain type of employee and I hire people who fit that profile. That is all I do. I get paid for every recruit who signs a contract. I admit I might know the country they'll be sent to, usually as security guards, but I'm never aware of the kind of deal that is going down. I don't need and I don't want to know."

"You can't be that ignorant, Black," Jeff said. "I'm sure you know that most of those jobs are illegal. Otherwise, why all the secrecy? Who are the people who hire your services?"

"I have no idea."

"Come on, you must know who your employer is. How are you contacted?"

"By e-mail."

"Who sends these e-mails and how are they signed?"

"They are never signed and I don't know who sends them."

"How do you contact them?"

Black shrugged. "By e-mail, how else."

"Then you have an address and a name?"

"No name. Just an e-mail address and it is not always the same."

"How do you get paid?" Jeff was beginning to get impatient.

"The money gets deposited to my bank. It is being transferred from a bank in the Cayman Islands."

That is the second time I hear about someone getting money from a bank in the Cayman Islands. Maybe Rob can find out the name of the bank. There must be a connection between these people and the people who sent twenty thousand dollars to Michael's account. "How do the men you hire get in touch with the company who hires them?"

"They don't. I give them an address where they're supposed to meet with a representative of that company."

"Perhaps you can give us one of those addresses?"

"I could but be assured, they are never the same. Just addresses of restaurants or other such public places." Black lifted his shoulders. "As you can see, I'm not at all directly involved. I'm just…"

"I know, I know. You're just a middleman. A business man who doesn't give a shit about our country, as long as you can make money." Jeff felt disgusted with the man's attitude. He looked at Rob. "You're the computer expert. Maybe you can find something on his computer that will help us trace the e-mails and eventually lead us to the people we're seeking."

"I can try." Rob moved behind the desk and sat down in the chair.

"Be careful with that computer," Black protested. "You might delete important information."

"Don't worry," Jeff assured him. "Rob is an expert. He knows more about computers than you, I'm sure."

Black gave a forced laugh. "That is not very comforting. I just know the basics."

Jeff watched Rob connect a flash drive to one of the ports in front of the tower. "This will only take a minute," Rob said.

Black heaved a deep sigh. "I knew I should not have come in this morning. That black cat crossing the street in front of me was not a good omen."

"Black cats are never a good omen," Jeff agreed, chuckling grimly. He remembered nearly stumbling over a black cat the day Michael was murdered. He was almost inclined to believe in these superstitions.

"Everything seems to be under control," Jerry said from his chair. "Maybe I can go home now?"

Jeff smiled at him. "Be patient, Jerry. It won't be long and we can all go home."

Rob rose from his seat. "That should do it. I think I have enough information." He walked past Black and padded him on the shoulder. "Everything you need is still on your computer. I took the liberty, though, to delete some stuff. I don't want you to send warnings to the good people you're dealing with."

"What the hell!" Black cursed. "What did I ever do to you guys? I'm running a valuable service here. Not everybody is squeamish about making money."

"We're not squeamish either, but there are some things we don't approve of. Selling out our country is one of them," Rob said, angrily. "Just think about how many American men have already been killed with weapons made in the US, weapons that should never have been in the hands of our enemies."

Jeff got up and followed Rob as he walked out of the door.

"What about our guns?" Black called after them.

"I'll take them to the cops. They'll get in touch with you and you can pick them up at your local police station." Rob chuckled to himself and murmured, "I hope they're registered."

Chapter Twelve

The flight back to Sacramento was uneventful. Rob and Jeff didn't discuss their visit to the recruiting office for fear of being overheard. Both men had no illusions about the dangers of dropping too much information in public. One small innocent remark could be picked up by the wrong party and create unpleasant consequences.

The plane landed in the late evening at the Sacramento International Airport and both men went separately through the gates, but they met outside the airport and took a taxi to Jeff's temporary quarters in the old warehouse.

"Stay in the taxi until I sweep the place," Rob told Jeff.

He came back about twenty minutes later. "All clear. It should be safe for you to stay here. At least for the moment. I'll be going to the military base in McClellan, but I'll be back in the morning."

The place looked abandoned, proof no one had stayed there while he was gone on his little excursion trip to Dallas. There was no food in the fridge, just a few bottles of beer, but since he'd eaten on the plane, he wasn't hungry. He hoped Rob would stock up the fridge in the morning and maybe even bring him some money.

He slept well. It wasn't home but better than a hotel room in a strange city.

Rob showed up early in the morning with a bag of groceries and a case of beer.

"I'm surprised you are still walking around free," Jeff said, smiling at the young man.

"Why?"

"I don't trust that Colonel O'Connor. He is out for blood. Any news from your father?"

Rob shook his head. "No, but I'm not worried. He'll get in touch when he deems it necessary. Like I told you, he's probably at his country home relaxing and working in his garden." He tilted his head. "Mind if I come in. This case is getting heavy."

Jeff chuckled and stepped aside. "Glad you came by. I worried I might have to drink beer for breakfast. There is no food in the fridge."

"I brought some, but I thought maybe we should go out for breakfast. I haven't eaten yet. That gruel they serve at the base is good enough for survival but not good enough for a gourmet like me." Rob put the beer bottles into the fridge. Then he took the food out of the bag. "I brought a few oranges. I thought you might like to eat some fresh fruit. The other stuff is all frozen dinners." He gave a quiet laugh. "I don't know how well you cook, sir. I won't be able to come every day to cook for you, and since there is no woman around to do it, you're better off with frozen stuff."

Jeff's thoughts clouded over. He thought of Kalila.

Rob seemed to sense Jeff's sudden change of sentiment. "Did I say something wrong?"

"No, I was just wondering about Kalila."

"She'll be fine. They have good doctors in Germany. They'll take care of her." His eyes rested on Jeff for a moment. "You are fond of her, sir?"

Jeff smiled. "She is a beautiful woman, Rob, and a caring human being."

"She may be that, but she is also a soldier. A very efficient soldier. We both saw her shoot that insurgent in the head. In cold blood and without flinching. May I also point out that she is a Muslim?"

"I know that." Jeff sighed. "I also realize we live in two different worlds, and not just physically, but that doesn't change the fact she is a very attractive woman."

"You've mentioned that already." Rob's smile teased him. "Don't get me wrong. I'd be the last guy to throw her out of my bed."

Jeff laughed. "You'd have to get her into it first, my young, horny friend." He became serious again. "I hope she recovers, that's all I'm saying."

"I hope so too, but now, let's go eat something. I'm starving."

"I won't argue with you on that."

Rob parked his car in one of the always-empty spots in the small parking lot beside the warehouse. The car looked clean and freshly washed.

"Aren't you afraid someone might steal this shiny car of yours?" Jeff asked, smiling.

Rob grinned and drove the blue VW out of the lot. "Car thieves want sports cars and expensive models. Volkswagens are not really at the top of the list. Not flashy enough. My car may not seem much, but you should know it has the latest versions of what technology has to offer these days, and more. It sports a GPS and a small camera built into the rear view mirror."

"What good is the camera if your vehicle is stolen and possibly crashed, destroying the tape or hard drive?"

"Don't worry, I thought of it and I fixed that problem. The camera transmits images of the people inside the car to a receiver in a secret location. Only I know where it is." He lowered his voice to a conspiratorial whisper, "You saw what I did in Baghdad. Well, I have the same surveillance technology at my disposal in my apartment. I can track this car anytime I need to."

"Is the camera transmitting now?"

"Of course it is. It turns on the moment someone enters this vehicle." He laughed gleefully. "This is the twenty-first century, sir. I was born to live it to its fullest and I take advantage of what technology lets me do."

"You love this, don't you? Spying on people, keeping track of their movements, listening in on their conversations?"

"Yes, I do. I've got spying in my blood."

"Some people might call you a Peeping Tom, possibly even a voyeur?"

"I don't watch people having sex, not intentionally, unless it is vital to my investigation." Rob grinned. "Watching isn't as much fun as doing it…the sex I mean." He glanced at Jeff. "That Iraqi woman…Kalila? Were you intimate with her?"

"You mean did I fuck her?" A stab of annoyance flashed through Jeff. He covered it up by saying 'fuck' instead of 'screw'.

"I guess that's what I mean. I wouldn't have put it so crudely though."

"If I did, it wouldn't be any of your business, Rob, but to answer your question, no, I didn't. Why the interest?"

Rob shrugged. "No particular reason. I'm just curious."

"Come on, Rob, don't give me that bullshit. You are more than curious. You must have a reason for asking me that. I know you too well."

"Well, okay." Rob didn't look at him as he maneuvered the small car through the traffic. "When two people like each other and get intimate, their objectives sometimes become somewhat clouded. Their judgment is off. You know the old saying about rose-colored glasses. We are keeping Lieutenant Ahmed under surveillance."

"Under surveillance? Why? And who is we?" Jeff felt irritated and realized that his feelings for Kalila may me stronger than he suspected. Even though they never had been intimate.

"She is an Iraqi, sir. A potential enemy. She might even be a spy. And since she is practically still on American soil, she needs to be watched. As to by whom? That is classified information."

Jeff threw him a sharp look. "What the hell are you implying, Rob? Am I also on the watch list?"

"Homeland Security has you on the list, but you have nothing to worry about from us, sir."

"Stop calling me 'sir', damn it! My name is Jeff. Call me by my name when we are not in public. I believe I've earned that."

"Okay. It's just that I was taught to treat my elders with respect." Rob smiled like a schoolboy.

"I'm forty-two years old. That doesn't make me an elder, for heaven's sake."

"It does in my book. You're almost as old as my father. In fact, you're old enough to be my father." Rob snickered good-humoredly. "By the way, I do have a lot of respect for you, and not just because of your age. I told you this before…you are a legend in the Corporation. A hero."

Jeff sighed. "Some hero. Aren't heroes supposed to be revered by the people? I'm a fugitive from the law, suspended from my job, listed as a potential threat to my country. That's not what I had envisioned when I was wounded defending this country and when I became a lawman."

"Good men are not rewarded for their deeds, sir. I mean Jeff. A good deed never goes unpunished, remember that."

"Who says that?"

"I'm not sure. Is it one of Murphy's laws, perhaps?" He slowed down his car. "There is a good place to eat," he said, searching for a spot to park. He found one not far away when another car pulled into the street, vacating a spot. They got out and walked the short distance to the restaurant.

The waitress who served them reminded Jeff a little of Connie. He made up his mind to drive to Fresno and see how she was doing, and possibly even talk to Detective Smith, one of the few people he still trusted. Perhaps he dug up some useful information. He knew that the young detective wasn't sitting idle. Smith was much too curious and ambitious for that.

When the waitress asked if they wanted separate bills, Rob told her to put it all on one. That decided it for Jeff.

"I want to talk to Morgan about giving me access to some funds, Rob. This is no way for me to carry on. I need my own money."

"Sure, we can do that. We'll drive to his office as soon as we're done here." Rob smiled. "I like your company, but I can't be with you all the time."

"I don't think I could stand it. After all, I should be hanging out with people my age. You're much too young for me. It's like spending time with my son...if I had one."

Rob smirked. "And I was beginning to think we were bonding."

Jeff laughed when he looked into Rob's innocent looking face. Hard to believe this was the same young man who executed a man in cold blood and without questions after Jeff gave him the order.

Jeff felt small pangs of guilt for his own role in that incident. Maybe he overreacted. Perhaps executing Lieutenant George Stiller had been a mistake. Perhaps. He wasn't sure anymore.

He looked around the café, at the people sitting in their chairs, eating bacon and eggs and muffins, drinking coffee, laughing. Businessmen and women, on their way to work or having breakfast with a client or friend. Men and women innocent of the knowledge that violence existed around them. Unaware of the men who tried to keep this violence away from them by committing violent acts themselves.

He had in effect murdered a soldier who at one time had defended his country, ready to give his life so others could live in peace. Just because Stiller had tried to make some extra money through means deemed criminal, Jeff condemned him to die.

How many of these business people had or would be committing crimes, like tax evasion, doing inside trading, cheating customers by selling them inferior products? Maybe even spying on the companies they worked for and selling the information to competitors. How many were lawyers who would defend a murderer and get him off on a technicality? Perfectly legal but a crime, nevertheless.

How many would go unpunished for their crimes?

Were these people any better than George Stiller? Was he?

He saw Rob watching him.

"Penny for your thoughts?" Rob said.

Jeff shook his head and smiled. "They're not worth even a penny. Too depressing."

The waitress came and brought their breakfast. He smiled at her and gazed at her slim hands as she poured his coffee. Looking up and into her face, he noticed the amusement in her almond eyes. *Am I getting so old that a young girl like her finds it amusing I might think her attractive?* "You're beautiful," he told her. "You remind me of a friend." It was not a lie.

"I've heard that line before," she said but smiled. "By the way, I have a boyfriend."

"Too bad." He let out an exaggerated sigh. "Just when I thought we had something going."

She laughed and walked away, hips swinging a little more than necessary.

"You old dog," Rob said, chuckling. "I think you should find yourself a hooker and get it out of your system."

"Get what out of my system?"

"You know. Fuck until you drop. I myself am always horny after finishing an assignment. It must be the adrenalin or something." Rob laughed and attacked his eggs.

"Did anyone ever tell you you're a comedian?" Jeff took a sip from his coffee and stared out of the window. It was a nice day outside. People were getting ready for the next day.

The Fourth of July. Independence Day.

We are taking our freedom for granted. Most people forget that it was a long struggle to make it possible. Let's hope we can celebrate this day forever.

* * * *

Morgan shook Jeff's hand and smiled jovially. "You look good with that beard and red hair. Great disguise. Your own mother wouldn't recognize you," he remarked. Then he squeezed his bulk back into the chair behind his oversized desk.

The desk looked cluttered with files. There was a pewter picture frame in one corner. Jeff wondered about the picture in the frame. Morgan's wife? His mistress? Sister? Did he have children? He didn't even know if the man was married.

"What can I do for you?"

Jeff cleared his throat. He felt like a teenager about to ask his dad for an allowance. "I don't want to sound ungrateful for your help, but I can't stay cooped up in that suite you've provided for me. I need to get out."

"Didn't you just get back from Dallas? And before that from Baghdad?" Morgan smiled. "That doesn't sound to me like a man who's cooped up."

"Maybe I didn't word it right. What I mean is I need to have access to money. I want to rent a car and drive down to Fresno."

"What's in Fresno?"

"A friend. Actually, two friends. One of them is a cop. I need to talk to him."

"A cop? I don't think that's wise, considering that you're a fugitive from the law."

"Nobody will recognize me." Jeff chuckled. "You said it yourself."

"You'll have to identify yourself to that cop. The other friend, I assume it's a woman?"

"Yes. Her name's Connie Wu. Her friend Dennis Kim was murdered a few weeks ago. Dennis was in my brother's outfit."

"She may be watched." Morgan rubbed his chin. "That cop friend of yours? How well do you know him?"

"I've met him during the investigation of my brother's murder. He showed a great deal of interest in the case, and I believe he won't betray me."

Morgan chuckled. "You believe that, but are you certain? He may be ambitious, and catching an enemy of the State might help him further his career. In addition, if he is so interested in your brother's case he most likely did some digging and attracted the attention of the wrong people.

He may also be watched closely."

"I'm aware of all those things, Captain Morgan, but I need to do something. Who else will? I need to find my brother's murderer and clear my own name in the process." Jeff had raised his voice. When he saw Morgan lifting his eyebrows, he let his shoulders slump and stepped back. "Sorry. Didn't mean to shout."

Morgan lifted a hand. "No need to apologize. I can imagine how you feel. You are right. Sitting in a room twiddling your thumbs won't help your case." Sighing and groaning, he got up and walked over to a safe in the corner of the office. Opening it, he pulled out an envelope and removed a credit card. He put the envelope back into the safe and locked it again.

He handed the card to Jeff. "Here, this will allow you to pull money from any banking machine. Just make sure you keep the amounts small in order not to raise any red flags. You can also use it to charge purchases of up to five hundred dollars." He went to his desk and scribbled something on a piece of paper. "This is your pin number to access the account."

Jeff put the card and the piece of paper into his wallet. "Thank you. I promise I won't misuse this privilege."

"Some of the money on this account is yours anyway. You earned it by going on the last mission. Uncle Sam does pay his employees, even if he sometimes doesn't know who they are."

"Who deposits this money and who is tracking the activity on this account?"

"Trusted army employees, but that's not really important." Morgan held out his hand. "Good luck with your investigation. Be careful." He looked at Rob who had said nothing all this time. "Watch your back, young man. Colonel O'Connor is on the warpath. He wants to bring down Grey Ops. Maybe it's time you started digging into his affairs. Something is going on and I have a feeling he is behind it. We need to take counter measures."

Rob nodded. "I'm already on it. Officially, I am on leave right now. It gives me the freedom to move around. I'll be flying to Washington tomorrow to find out more about the Colonel. A friend of mine is stationed near Washington. Maybe he can fill me in on a few things."

"Good. Now I must get back to work." Morgan smiled. "I'm

defending a large corporation accused of tax evasion. It may not be an exciting case but quite lucrative."

* * * *

Rob took Jeff to a car rental agency and left. The car Jeff rented was not new and not flashy. He didn't need to draw attention to himself and the car he was driving.

My red beard is flashy enough.

He left shortly after lunch and came to the outskirts of Fresno at around four o'clock, just in time to be caught up in the evening rush hour.

When he arrived at the apartment building Connie lived in, he parked his car a couple of blocks away and walked back to the building. Since he didn't want to announce himself, he waited by the door until someone opened it and quickly slipped into the foyer.

Connie lived on the fourth floor and he decided to use the stairs instead of the elevator. He hoped she was home, but when he knocked on the door and she didn't open up, he realized she wasn't.

He waited at the end of the corridor, watching the elevator. She stepped out of it about thirty minutes later. When she saw him, she slowed down for a moment, but then she shrugged and walked on.

To avoid scaring her, he called out in a low voice when he was still about halfway down the corridor. "Hi, Connie."

Startled, she looked up and put her hands over her mouth.

"It's me, Connie," he said softly. "Jeff."

"Jeff?" She stared into his face, not recognizing him.

"Jeff Chartrand. I'm hiding behind this red beard."

Her face suddenly lit up and then she was in his arms. "Jeff, Jeff! What are you doing here?" She looked around, up and down the corridor, as if expecting someone to appear.

"Looking for you," he said.

She pulled him toward the door to her apartment. "We'd better get inside," she whispered. She fumbled with the lock.

"Let me help," he said, taking the keys from her trembling fingers.

Once inside her apartment, she moved into his arms again and kissed him hungrily. "I thought you were dead or something," she sobbed. "I was really worried when I saw you picture all over the news."

He looked into her tearstained face and smiled. "As you can see I'm very much alive."

She touched his cheek and stroked his beard. "I never knew you had red hair."

Laughing, he disengaged himself from her embrace. "I don't, but I'm told it makes me look sophisticated."

She took his hand and pulled him toward the couch. "Come, sit down while I take a quick shower and change out of these clothes. These slacks are glued to my legs. It's so damned hot outside and the air-conditioning in my car isn't working. Want me to get you a drink?"

"You go and get changed. I'll get my own drink."

He watched her disappear into the bathroom. He found a glass, got some ice from the freezer and walked over to her small liqueur cabinet and poured himself a double Scotch.

Sitting on the couch, sipping his drink, he heard the water running in the bathroom. He closed his eyes and relaxed. Listening to the sound of the water, feeling the softness of the cushion behind his back and inhaling the hint of Connie's perfume still lingering in the air, made him feel at peace.

Why couldn't things always be this way? Why didn't everybody want to live in peace and just enjoy life? Why were some people so consumed by hatred that they wanted nothing else but build weapons and bombs and use them to murder other human beings?

"Come and dance with me, my Darling." She did a little pirouette in front of him and kicked up her long legs. He laughed and pulled her to him. "You are so beautiful, Nicole. I don't think I could ever live without you." She smiled, her green eyes suddenly sad. "Neither could I without you." She pressed her lips against his. They felt warm and soft.

He opened his eyes, disoriented for a moment. Dark, almond eyes looked into his.

"Did you fall asleep?" Connie smiled down at him.

"I guess I dozed off." Her kimono was open and he saw that she wore a transparent negligee, which didn't hide much of her lovely form underneath. Her breasts swung freely in front of his face.

"I thought we should celebrate your return," she whispered. Then she began unbuttoning his shirt.

Groaning, he let her undress him, let her pull down his pants. He was ready for her and she chuckled when she circled her fingers around his manhood.

She didn't wear any panties and her thighs opened when he slid on top of her.

Crying out softly, she took him into her and moved against him with unrestrained passion.

"I've missed you," she moaned. "I've missed feeling you inside me. Let me take off my kimono and this silly little thing. I want to feel your chest against my naked breasts." She shrugged out of her kimono, pulled the sheer negligee over her head and threw it onto the floor. Naked, she molded her body into his.

He tasted her sweet kisses, explored her mouth with his tongue. She wrapped her legs around his torso, pressed her heels into his buttocks and clung to him as he moved steadily between her clutching thighs.

Soft, oh so soft.

How can anything create such heavenly pleasure?

Climbing toward the peak of the mountain of pure ecstasy, he made her reach hers before he attained his. Her jubilant whimpers reverberated like music inside his mind, strumming his pleasure center like the fingers of a skilled instrumentalist.

Her fingernails raking his back amplified his need for release, and when it came, he let out a shout of triumph and satisfaction. The descent from the summit was gradual, as they lay exhausted in each other's arms, breath coming in great gasps, damp and hot from the strain.

He closed his eyes again, enjoying her warm body underneath him, her soft thighs circling his hips, her breasts against his chest.

"I love you," she whispered into his ear. Then she kissed him on the nose and relaxed her thighs.

"I wish we could stay like this forever," he murmured.

She chuckled. "You are getting heavy. I don't think I could last that long."

Reluctantly, he let her go and sat up.

"I think the pillow you pushed under my butt needs to be washed," she said, laughing. "We sure made a mess of it."

He joined her laughter. "You've made a mess of it. I don't think I've ever made love to a woman as passionate as you."

"Really? And how many were there, if I may ask?" She put her naked toes into his lap. "Maybe I should ask *him*?"

"Very funny." He took her foot between his hands. "You have beautiful feet, so small and nicely formed."

"I take care of them." She wiggled her toes.

"Do all oriental girls have small feet? I hear it is supposed to be a sign of beauty."

She shrugged. "They don't bind young girl's feet anymore, if that's what you mean."

"I don't think they ever did in this country." He lifted her foot and planted a wet kiss on her big toe.

"Have you made love to an oriental girl before?" she asked.

"You're the first one."

"I've never made love to a white man. You are the first."

He chuckled. "Actually, you still haven't made love to a white man. Not a full-blooded one anyway. I'm half Sioux. The other half is of French ancestry."

"Oh, I didn't know that. I mean about the Sioux part."

"I don't advertise it. Does it matter?"

"No. Why should it? I love you the way you are, even with your red beard."

He grinned. "You like it? Just so you know...my name is Dr. Richard Raymond Callwell."

"Doctor?"

"A chiropractor. From Toronto in Canada." When she daintily lifted an eyebrow, he grinned. "That's right, I'm a Canadian."

"I've never made love to a Canadian either. Before today." She giggled.

"Technically you still haven't."

"Oh, shut up." She pulled her foot away and sat up. "How long are you staying?"

He shrugged. "I hadn't thought about it."

"Tomorrow is the Fourth of July. I'm not working. We could spend the time in bed and make love all day."

"We could." He grinned, feeling like a teenager, reckless and eager to explore a new world that had suddenly opened up for him...a world of pleasure and excitement.

"Hungry?" she asked.

"Yes, as a matter of fact, I am."

She rose. "I'll make us something to eat, but first I have to clean up and get dressed again." She headed for the bathroom.

He watched her plump buttocks as they gently moved when she walked away from him. "I like you the way you are," he called after her. "Naked."

"I'm sure you do." Laughing, she disappeared into the bathroom.

Picking up her negligee and kimono from the floor, he folded them and put them on the coffee table. He didn't think she'd need them for the rest of the night.

When she came out of the bathroom, she said, "Why don't you take a shower while I prepare supper." Then she went into her bedroom to get dressed.

Feeling grimy and tired, he followed her suggestion. A shower would be refreshing and benefit him greatly. It might even wash away this feeling of anxiety that had hung over him these last few weeks. The calm happiness he experienced in Connie's embrace had dissipated and the anxiety returned.

He could hear her humming in the bedroom and it pleased him to know that he was the reason for her pleasant mood. It would be nice to spend a couple of days with her and keep that moment alive for little while.

Chapter Thirteen

"Do you know what time it is?"

Jeff opened an eye and turned his head to look sleepily at Connie. "What time is it?"

"Almost eleven. In the morning. And it is a beautiful morning. We've missed most of it already."

He opened his other eye. "How can you be so cheerful? Aren't you tired?"

"No." She laughed happily. "Making love never tires me." She pushed back the covers and stretched. Then she slipped from the bed.

Jeff watched her as she padded to the window and opened the blinds. Then he squinted at the silhouette of her petite naked body outlined against the bright light streaming in through the window. She looked like a beautiful dream vision. "Are you an angel or a demoness come to torture me?" he asked, sitting up.

She laughed again. "I am whatever you like me to be." She came back to the bed and hovered over him.

He stared at her bare breasts. "You are a temptress," he groaned.

She bent and planted a quick kiss on his lips. "Come on and get up. You don't want to waste this day in bed. It is too beautiful for that. Listen to the birds singing outside. They are calling *Come on sleepyhead*."

"You've sucked the life out of my poor body and now I just want to go back to sleep."

Grabbing his feet, she pulled. "A cold shower will make you feel better." She looked at him from under lowered lids. "If you're a good boy there may be another night of pure pleasure and ecstasy waiting for you, but first you and I will celebrate the Fourth of July as it should be celebrated. There'll be fireworks in the park. I'd like to go there."

"All right, but give me a few more minutes to wake up. You go and have that shower." He pulled the covers back over his nude body and closed his eyes.

Am I getting too old for these all-nighters?

He smiled remembering their furious lovemaking. She sure was full of fire and passion and he was looking forward to another night with her.

Strange how things sometimes develop. Ten years of celibacy and no desire for the company of a woman or sex, and now he couldn't get enough. Connie awakened something in him that had been asleep for much too long. Maxine added fuel to the fire inside him and given him the idea that something might develop between them. And Kalila? Mysterious and hauntingly beautiful Kalila? He never did get a chance to taste her passion, and that made her that much more desirable, but he knew that Connie was the one who stilled his yearning. There was more between them than just desire and sex.

Much more.

He realized he had fallen in love.

She came out of the bathroom, naked and smiling. He felt the desire burning in him to take her into his arms and cover her delectable petite body with his kisses.

She must have seen it in his eyes, because she lifted a finger in a scolding gesture, like a mother about to lecture her child. "No more hanky panky," she said, her dark eyes laughing at him. "Go, be a good boy and take your shower."

He got out of bed and walked toward her, about to take her into his arms, but she stepped back. "Shower!" She wrinkled her nose. "The air smells stale in here." Then she giggled. "I wonder why. I better open the window to bring in some fresh air."

Slapping her on one round buttock, he headed for the bathroom.

The water caressed his skin like soft rain on a warm summer evening, and he reveled in the feeling of peace and happiness it washed through his body. It didn't only clean his skin but also his mind. He thought of the desert in Kuwait, where water was scarce and a commodity, not to be wasted in such a mundane manner as taking a long shower. Water was more precious than oil and yet, it was oil that caused many of the problems of the twenty-first century.

Water was necessary for the survival of every living creature on Earth, but oil fueled civilization. Oil made it possible to travel from one place to another in comfort and in a short time. Oil provided means of heating homes, opened the sky and possibly the road to the stars. But oil exacted a terrible price. It polluted the air, the water, the soil. It caused conflict over who should own it and who should control its flow.

Many people thought it was religion that was the cause of all evil, but was it?

Jeff didn't know but suspected that oil was a greater threat to the survival of the human race than ideologies.

Religion had caused many wars in the past, but this was a new century. Oil was the new religion. The new god. The people who controlled the flow of oil used religion as an excuse to arouse passion and hatred between people of different faiths, hoping nobody would notice that the real reason was not religion but oil.

"Have you fallen asleep in there?"

Connie's voice broke into his thoughts, brought him back to reality. He decided not to think about anything but her for the time he was going to spend with her.

There would be nothing but happiness and good feeling.

He shut off the spray of water and stepped out of the shower. Connie stood there, dressed in a blouse and tight slacks. She handed him a towel, smiling up at him. "I love you," he said, looking into her dark eyes.

"Wow!" She chuckled. "I love you too." Then she lifted up and kissed him on the lips.

He took her into his arms and held her tightly.

After a while, she pushed against his chest. "You're getting me all wet." She stepped out of his embrace. "Are you feeling all right?"

He laughed softly and touched her face. "I'm feeling better than I've felt for a long time. Thanks to you."

"I'm glad. For a moment there I thought something was wrong. Come on, I'll make us breakfast, even though it's late. I don't have much at home, just some toast. I could cook you an egg, if you want. We can go out later for a larger meal."

"An egg and toast will be fine. And a cup of coffee. Black and no sugar."

"Coming up. Now, dry yourself and get dressed before I give in to my urges and drag you back to bed."

He leered at her. "Give in to your urges. I don't mind."

"You have no willpower, Dr. Richard Callwell. Chiropractor from Canada. I can't wait until you're Jeff Chartrand again. I liked him better. He wasn't such a sex-maniac." Laughing, she left the bathroom.

He grinned at his image in the mirror. "You heard the lady, Dr. Callwell. No sex until tonight. So control yourself."

The aroma of brewing coffee reminded him of breakfasts with Nicole. So long ago. He had been happy then. They both had been happy. He realized he needed to forget the past and go on with his life, not compare things to the way they had been, not to remember the old memories but to create new ones.

He was determined to do that.

When he walked into the kitchen he noticed the tablecloth on the table. Connie even lit a couple of candles. A cooked egg sat inside a small holder, a tiny spoon and a knife lay on a napkin. Two slices of toast on a plate. A container with jam and another one with butter stood in the middle of the table.

She poured his coffee into a cup made from delicate porcelain. Then she poured her own. He sat down, across from her, almost afraid to pick up the cup with his thick fingers.

Nicole never set a table like this. She preferred to drink coffee from a mug. It never mattered to him; he drank coffee from a paper cup, if necessary, but he had to admit, this was nice.

"Do you always eat this way?" he asked, peeling the top of his egg.

"What do you mean?"

"This fancy cup, silver cutlery, a table cloth, candles?"

She smiled. "Only with someone special…like a lover."

"Are you doing this a lot?"

Her smile vanished. "These dishes have collected dust for a long time. And the candles have never been lit."

"I'm sorry, I didn't mean it that way."

She reached across the table to touch his hand. "I'm really happy you came, even though you are taking a chance to come here."

"I had to see you, Connie. I've missed you. I never realized how much until last night."

"I've missed you too. When you didn't come to the funeral I thought you didn't really care, but then I saw your picture in the paper and on television. They said you have ties to Al Queda and that you shot some people. How much of that is true."

He buttered his toast but ignored the jam. "I shot a couple of people who deserved it. I also shot Ethan Grey…in self-defense. The rest is fabrication."

He saw her hand go to her mouth. "You shot Ethan Grey? But he was…"

"…one of the Ten Commandos, I know." Jeff stared at her. "Someone gave him the order to kill me. They also made it look as if he were an assassin. He carried an attaché case with pictures of Dennis, Toby Miller, and others."

"Are you saying he killed Dennis?"

"That's what everyone was supposed to believe. I don't buy it. What reason would he have? No, he was set up."

"And you? Were you also set up?"

"No. I followed a lead, but some people don't want me to dig. They want me dead."

"Homeland Security among them?"

He shrugged. "I don't know. Did you know that John MacKay had a brother? A twin? His name is Dave MacKay and he works for Homeland Security."

"John MacKay was killed shortly after Darrin Montana died. Maybe his brother thinks Michael and the others had something to do with his killing."

"Why would he think that?"

"Dennis touched on the subject once. I remember him saying that John MacKay didn't deserve to die the way he did. No man did. He didn't elaborate and I never asked." Her face expressed concern. "Is it possible that Dave MacKay is behind it all? He does have the connections and the means to do it. These guys from Homeland Security have way too much power as far as I'm concerned."

Jeff shook his head. "I don't know. I didn't care much for the way agent MacKay treated me, but somehow I doubt that he is mixed up in this whole affair. At least not just him. There are more players involved, much more powerful players than Dave MacKay. People who have ties to the government. I don't believe that revenge is the motive for the murder of my brother or any of the other members of his unit."

He paused and sipped from his coffee. "I can't tell you more for fear of putting you in danger. Sorry."

She stared at him. "You do know something, don't you?"

"Nothing concrete." He smiled. "Remember the first time we met I told you that I'm not a conspiracy buff. Well, let me just say maybe now I am."

"Where have you been all this time, Jeff? They had you in custody. How did you get away?"

"The less you know the safer you'll be, Connie. I've already given you too many hints."

She sighed. "Maybe you're right. Maybe I shouldn't know what you're involved in. By the way, I never told you that Brian McGee came to see me."

"McGee, the one who according to Dennis saw it all? Whatever it was. What did he want?"

"He is scared for his life. I've never seen a man who was afraid of every shadow that loomed over him. He gave me an envelope. To be opened upon his demise."

"What's in the envelope?" Jeff stared at her, anxious to find out more. To see Connie may not have been the only reason for him coming here. Fate sometimes works that way.

"I don't know. I promised him not to open it until I had to. I told him I hoped it would not be for a long time." Her eyes searched his face. "Do you think I should open it?"

"Maybe it contains important information about the murders. We might possibly be able to save his life."

"I want nothing to do with it. You can have the envelope and do with it what you think is necessary." Her eyes had a sudden haunted look in them. "I am afraid, Jeff."

"Maybe you should move. Away from Fresno. Away from all this. I have a friend who could give you a new identity."

"Where could I move to? Fresno is my home. This is where I grew up. I have my career here, and I like this city. Can your friend offer me a life as good as I have now? Can he give me instant friends?" Her hand shook when she picked up her cup ."Can he guarantee my safety?"

"Your safety, yes, but the rest?" He shrugged. "Only time can provide you with that."

"Right. And I don't believe a new identity will keep me safe. If these people are as powerful as you say and have ties to the government, I won't be safe, unless I move out of the country, and even then…" She dabbed at her eyes. "No, Jeff, I must stay here and hope you and your friends can find who's behind all this and bring the guilty ones to justice."

"Believe me, I want nothing more than that. I just worry about you. I never did ask you. Have you spoken to Detective Smith since the funeral?"

"I have. After these guys from Homeland Security came for a visit."

"Shit! You never told me about that."

She smiled at his outburst. "You never gave me a chance. We haven't talked much until now."

He smiled back. "We talked, but not with words. My favorite way of talking." He became serious. "What did they want?"

"They asked about Dennis. I don't think I told them anything new. They wanted to know if Dennis had some papers, pictures, diaries. Stuff like that."

"Did you tell them about us?" he asked anxiously.

"No. I didn't think it was any of their business. They never asked."

"Good. Then it was just a routine visit. They came to fish. The less they know the better." He let out a small breath of relief. Perhaps they would leave Connie alone after this. He didn't really believe it but even bulldogs give up sometimes.

"I'm not a naïve little girl, Jeff. Living with Dennis taught me a few things. For instance, never volunteer information to any government agency. Only answer what is asked, nothing more."

"Smart girl. Don't trust anyone. Especially the government."

"That sounds strange coming from a cop." Her lips smiled faintly.

"I know the routine. One innocent remark might bite you in the ass later." He looked around the apartment. "I don't see any of the pictures I saw last time decorating the walls."

Connie smiled. "Those pictures and paraphernalia belonged to Dennis. He's gone now and I figured I'd put my own touch to the apartment."

"What did you do with his things?"

"I put them into his bedroom. I don't have the heart to throw them out…not yet." She lifted her hands in an apologetic gesture.

"Doesn't he have any relatives?"

"A sister. In New York. She never showed much interest in him. I don't think she ever forgave him for being gay."

Jeff nodded but didn't comment on that. It was not easy for most straight parents to accept that their son or daughter was gay. Siblings might be more inclined to at least tolerate a gay brother or sister, but sometimes even they refused to do so. He tried to be open-minded in accepting the fact that others existed who preferred a different lifestyle, but he wasn't sure how he would have reacted had he found out Michael was a homosexual. "What about parents?"

"They're both dead."

"How about you? Any siblings? Parents?"

"I have two sisters. Ashley lives in San Francisco. She is a model and moves around a lot. My other sister, Lin, married a guy from Hawaii."

"You could move there. Hawaii is a beautiful place."

Connie let out a little laugh. "She's ten years older than me. Her husband is an idiot. He made a pass at me on their wedding day. I was seventeen. No, thank you. It would never work."

"And your parents?"

"I never knew my father. My mother died of an overdose when I was three." She shrugged. "I ended up in a foster home and ran away when I turned fourteen. Don't ask me how I survived."

Jeff looked at her for a moment. "You've had a rough life, but you turned out all right." He smiled. "Better then many people I know."

She dabbed at her eyes, sniffing. Then she laughed. "Let's not talk about the past. I want to enjoy this day with you. You want to go for a walk in the park?"

He nodded. "Sure. Sounds like a good idea."

They left the apartment an hour later. It was hot outside...hotter than it had been for many years in July.

"We could use some rain," Connie remarked.

"Not today, I hope." He put his arm around her waist and pulled her a little closer. Her slim body felt light against his arm as she walked beside him, her hip touching his. "They've got flooding in the southern states. Let's enjoy the warm dry weather we're having."

"I am, but rain would help the forest fire situation." She laughed happily. "But you're right. Not today." She leaned her head against his shoulder.

There were not many people walking around because of the heat. They wouldn't come out until dark to watch the fireworks.

"Let's go feed the ducks," Connie suggested and pulled him toward one of the ponds in the park. They stopped by one of the vendors and bought some popcorn. Connie threw the popped kernels into the small flock of ducks swimming on the water and laughed when the ducks fought over them.

Jeff sat on a park bench, watching her, enjoying the view of her slim body, her graceful movements. *She's like a swan, but I bet she was never an ugly duckling.*

She joined him on the bench, her cheeks flushed from the heat and the excitement. Touching his hand, she said, "This is the best Fourth of July I ever celebrated."

He smiled and squeezed her hand. "Mine too."

When a group of screaming children came running over the lawn toward the pond, Connie laughed. "I think it's time to move on. Those ducks are noisy enough."

"I'm going to visit Detective Smith tomorrow," Jeff said, as they walked down one of the paths.

"He's a cop," Connie said, shaking her head. "I don't know. He may turn you in. That's his job."

"Not Smith. He wouldn't do that."

They stood underneath a grove of trees. Connie lifted up and kissed him gently. "I wish all this would go away and you and I could be together like two ordinary people. I wish none of this bad stuff ever happened."

"So do I, but then we may have never met. Sometimes bad things bring good things." He kissed her back and held her for a moment, his eyes closed, tasting the freshness of her mouth and inhaling her feminine scent.

They broke apart when they heard voices.

"I love you," he whispered. "Everything will turn out all right. You must believe that."

Chapter Fourteen

The next morning, Connie went back to work "Lock up when you leave," she told Jeff. "And don't forget to take the key I put on the counter."

He chuckled and kissed her. "Don't worry. I'll see you tonight."

He left the apartment a couple of hours later and drove to the precinct where Detective Smith worked. He knew he might be taking a chance, but he firmly believed he could trust the young detective.

Smith, of course, didn't recognize him when he walked up to his desk.

"Can I help you?" the young detective asked. "By the way, how did you get past the desk sergeant?"

Jeff grinned. "I told him I'm your cousin and I have to discuss a family matter with you."

Smith narrowed his eyes and stared at Jeff. "I don't remember a cousin with red hair, but your voice, it sounds familiar."

Jeff handed him a note and waited until the detective read it. He smiled when Smith stared at him. "Let's go across the street. I'll buy you a cup of coffee."

"Okay." Jeff nodded. "I could use a cup."

They didn't talk as they crossed the busy street. Once inside the restaurant, Smith said in a low voice, "What the hell are you thinking, Jeff? You're a wanted man. Apparently, Homeland Security is looking for you. Someone sprung you from custody under false pretenses. Where have you been? What are you involved in?"

Jeff smiled thinly, registering Smith's use of his first name. "Seems you're keeping up-to-date, Marvin. Let me ask you a question first. Are you going to turn me in?"

Smith regarded him in silence. "I told you once that you needed a friend. I am that friend. No, I'm not going to turn you in, but you must tell me everything you know."

"Last time we saw each other I asked you if you wanted to be a part of this. I'm asking you again, just to make sure. You still want to be mixed up with me?"

"Yes, I do. Now more so than ever."

"Your life may be in danger if you do. The murder of my brother is just part of this whole thing. I still don't know who's doing the killing, but I know now that my brother may have been not the innocent victim I thought he was. I have information that he was involved in selling weapons to insurgents."

Smith let out a low whistle. "That's big. Are you telling me the Military is involved?"

Jeff nodded. "It seems that way." He bent across the table. "I'm putting my life into your hands, Marvin, but I trust you. I just came back from Iraq. We stopped one of these weapons transactions and took out a number of insurgents. Now my head is even further on the chopping block." He chuckled. "That's why the disguise. I need to stay free so I can keep on digging, but I can't do it alone. The more people on my side the better my chances of finding out what this is all about."

"You can count on me, my friend."

"I never doubted that but be careful. I don't want to be responsible for the sudden end of your promising career."

"I wouldn't be the man I am if I would always play it safe." Smith smiled. "You seem to be putting your head between a crocodile's jaws constantly and until now you've survived. I will, too." His green eyes studied Jeff. "Tell me about Iraq."

Jeff shook his head. "I can't go into details. Just telling you about me being there constitutes a break in regulations."

"Whose regulations? The army's?" Smith leaned back and folded his arms across his chest. "You are a cop," he mused. "Before you became a cop you served in the Military. You were wounded in Kuwait January 19, 1991. Discharged from the army with a medal for bravery. A Purple Heart."

Jeff watched the young man. "I never told you that about me."

"I'm good at what I do, Jeff. I checked you out." Smith stopped talking when the waitress came to refill his cup.

"Will there be anything else?" she asked.

He shook his head. "Thank you, Gloria. We're fine." He waited until she moved to the next booth and looked at Jeff. "There is more. You were suspended from your job. Then you went and had a shootout with a man named Galliano, presumably a mobster. You killed him during this shootout. You were arrested but released into the custody of the Military. Why?" His green eyes shone brightly. "Why would the Military do that?"

Jeff smiled. "Maybe I have friends in the Military."

"I'm sure you do. However, that is not it. You told me you were in Iraq on a mission." Smith drummed his fingers on the tabletop. "You are not even in the army anymore. Why would they send you on a mission? Wait a minute. This goes back more than sixteen years. To your early days in the army."

He stared. "Wow! Now I get it. Your were a member of a special unit. A *Ghost Unit*. You still are. You, my friend, are a ghost! A *Spook*."

"Careful what you are implying." Jeff kept his voice neutral.

"I'm implying nothing, just thinking out loud. I want to make a point here. If I can come to this conclusion, others can." Smith sipped from his cup, slurping noisily, his eyes on Jeff. He put it down and rubbed his hands. "This is exciting. I love a mystery."

"That's all it is, a mystery," Jeff said.

"Not anymore. I see things clearly now, my friend. I don't use the word 'friend' carelessly because I consider you my friend. You need my help. You weren't the only one I investigated. For instance, did you know that Galliano is related to Anthony Mariano?"

"Who's Anthony Mariano?"

"He's the Godfather of the Chicago Mafia."

Jeff let that piece of information sink in. It was his turn to say, "Wow!"

"That's not all," Smith continued. "There are rumors that Larkin might be running for office of President of the United States."

"He's an ambitious and charismatic man," Jeff commented. "He might make a good president."

"He is an oilman. He may be inclined to keep the conflict in the Middle East going. It would be in his best interest and the interest of every oilman in the country. Oil prices have been rising. Oil companies have been raking in enormous profits. They like to keep it that way.

Controlling the flow of oil is of utmost importance to future prices.

"This push for more fuel efficient vehicles and the switch to ethanol will shrink profits for the oil companies unless they can raise the price of crude oil. Only by reducing the supply will they be able to accomplish that. Oil will be in demand for a long time still."

Jeff chuckled. "You should have become an economist, Marvin. Or an analyst, not a cop."

"My analytical mind makes me a better detective. It gives me the ability to connect people and events that others might overlook." Smith glanced at his watch. "I'd better get back to the office. My captain might become curious." He held out a hand. "Take care, Jeff, my friend, and be careful. Keep in touch. By the way, how is Miss Wu?"

Jeff took the offered hand and held it for a moment. "She's fine. You can get in touch with her if anything develops and you need to talk with me. She will forward your message." He smiled. "You be careful, too, my friend."

Smith rose, but Jeff decided to stay and have another cup of coffee.

He mulled over what Smith had told him about Galliano. It may mean nothing, but it also might mean that Galliano had ties to the Chicago mob. He didn't know what to think. He decided to drive home the next day. He needed to speak to Montana.

He corrected himself.

Maxine. After all, they had been intimate and were on first name basis. At least in private.

Thinking of her made him feel guilty. Until now, it had always been the memory of Nicole preventing him from searching out other women. That had suddenly changed. Maybe it was a good thing.

He finished his coffee and drove back to Connie's apartment. Since there wasn't much for him to do, he went into Dennis Kim's bedroom to see if he could find anything useful. It felt strange searching through a dead man's things, as if snooping around in a man's life and disturbing his memory. He shrugged. He was a cop and this was not the first time he had to go through another person's private possessions.

He looked at the pictures. This was all that was left of a man who had given his life for his country. Not in combat but in the aftermath. He had seen something he wasn't supposed to see. Or maybe even been part of something which, were it publicly known, could put certain people in danger. And for that, he was murdered. Jeff was certain of that.

Just like Michael.

Connie came home earlier than he expected, and he was happy to see her.

"Come into the shower with me," she said, while she took off her clothes.

Looking at her naked body made up his mind and he stepped into the small cubicle with her. Lathering each other with scented soap, they soon were thrashing around in the cramped space, locked together.

Her pert buttocks moved in his hands as she thrust them back and forth. Moaning, she gasped, "Let's go to bed and continue in a more comfortable place."

Laughing, they dried each other with one towel then they stumbled onto the bed, on top of the covers. Her slim thighs parted and he fell between them, his erect penis searching for an entrance into her luscious body. She gave a little cry when he slid deep into her hot sheath and churned her lower body underneath him furiously.

His hands held her buttocks as he thrust into her with powerful strokes.

"You're a sex-starved nympho," he told her when they lay in each other's arms, exhausted and breathing hard.

She laughed coyly. "And you're a sex-maniac. Let's go out for supper. I feel like eating a huge juicy steak."

She took him to a fancy place. He was proud to be her escort. She looked absolutely stunning in her green dress. When they followed the waiter and she walked in front of him, her buttocks moved deliciously under the tight material, and he was sure she didn't wear any panties.

He couldn't wait to take her home again.

"You are the sexiest woman I have ever met," he told her during dinner.

She laughed and winked at him. "You're just saying that because you want me in your bed."

"I don't have a bed."

"I guess then you'll have to join me in mine."

When they arrived back home, she was a little tipsy and giggled a lot.

"Let me dance for you," she said.

"Go ahead." He watched her put a CD into the player, anxious to see her dance. He remembered the last time she had done that.

No woman had ever danced for him. Connie was the only one and she was good at it. She twisted her body with sensuous movements in front of him. Taking off her necklace, she put it on the table, looking back over her shoulder as she walked away from him. Then she turned and removed first one shoe and then the other.

Pulling he hem of her dress halfway up her slim thighs, she pretended to roll down her non-existent stockings.

Laughing, she lifted the hem and slipped the dress over her head, slowly exposing the rest of her body.

He had been right. She didn't wear any panties under her tight dress, not even a bra.

They made love on the carpet, in front of the fireplace. It was only an electric fireplace but it added to the romantic atmosphere.

She fell asleep in his arms, and he carried her to bed.

Morning came much too soon.

* * * *

"Are you sure you want to leave?" she asked.

He stroked her hair. "As much as I would like to stay here forever, I have to go. I'm a fugitive from the law and eventually they will find me. I want to solve the murder of my brother, of Dennis, and the other men in their unit. I need to clear my name and establish my innocence in the shooting of that fat pig Galliano. I want my old life back."

She smiled sadly. "That will never happen, Jeff. I'm part of your life now or don't you want me in your life?"

"Of course I do." He kissed her. "I don't ever want you out of my life again. I love you."

"And I love *you*." She rolled into his arms. "Come, make love to me one more time."

"Won't you be late for work?"

"I'll go in later. This is more important than work." She touched him and laughed. "I see you are not exactly fighting my suggestion."

He chuckled and moaned as she sheathed him.

"You feel good," she breathed. "Let's not hurry."

It was almost ten o'clock by the time they got out of bed. After showering, Connie made him breakfast.

"Take care," she whispered into his ear when they finally said good-bye to each other. "And come back soon." She handed him a large envelope. "This is the envelope McGee gave me. Take it."

He stopped for lunch in a small place called Chowchilla. It was already past two o'clock, and he decided to call his sister Barbara from a payphone. Payphones were not easy to track; at least he hoped that was the case.

Barbara picked up the phone on the second ring. "Hello?"

"Hi, Sis."

After a gasp and a short pause, she said in a small voice, "Jeff?"

"In the flesh." He chuckled. "Actually not on your end. Just my voice, but I'm still alive."

"We were so worried when we saw your picture all over the news. Are you all right? It's been over a month since we heard from you. We didn't know what to think. Where are you? Are you phoning from jail?"

He laughed. "Not from jail, but I can't tell you where I am in case you're phone is bugged."

"My phone bugged? Come on, Jeff. Now you're paranoid. Who would bug my phone?"

"I don't know and I'm not saying it is. I just don't want to take any chances."

"Are you coming home?"

"No, I can't."

"I wish you would come home. A man with a heavy accent phoned last week. He wants to know where he can find you. Is it starting all over again, Jeff?"

"What else did this man say?"

"He threatened to do harm to our family. Jeff, can't you do anything to stop this?"

Jeff was ready to smash the phone into a wall. When was this going to stop? "Have you talked to the police?" He asked even though he knew what her answer would be.

"They won't help. Even your friend Maxine says she can't do anything unless she knew who this man was. Oh, Jeff, this is so frustrating. I'm scared." A little sob escaped her into the phone, making him even angrier at the men who were behind the terrorization of his family.

"I'll see what I can do. I promise. I had better hang up, Barb. Give my love to the girls and say *Hi* to Helmut. Tell him we'll share a bottle of his German beer some day again. I love you."

"Don't hang up, Jeff. There something else I need to tell you. Remember the little boy you told me about? Michael's son? You won't believe this, but he is living with us now. Two men came and brought him. They had all the necessary papers. Everything is legal. He is such a sweet little boy and so bright. He already knows many words in English. Helmut is really exited. He finally has a son."

Jeff couldn't help but smile over her enthusiasm. He knew they had done the right thing. Barbara would make a good mother to him and Helmut a good father. "I'm happy to hear that," he said.

"You don't sound very excited." She sounded disappointed.

"Believe me, I am excited. Keep him safe. He is the only one to carry Michael's name and the Chartrand genes. I'd better go. Don't let that man with the accent bother you. Bye." He hung up.

Fuck it! Those guys just didn't give up. He needed to find out who that caller was, before he did something stupid. Obviously, he was one of the people who threatened him before. Taking out their connections in Iraq seemed to have done nothing but infuriate them. They needed to be stopped.

It was evening when he arrived in Sacramento. He drove back to his temporary residence in the old warehouse and decided to get in touch with Barbara the next day. He left his rented car in the small parking lot, hoping it would still be there when he needed it in the morning.

The next day, he drove to Barbara's residence but parked his car a couple of blocks away. One could never be too careful. He walked up to one of the boys who played ball in the back lane behind Barbara's house and asked him if he wanted to make a few bucks. Then he handed him a sealed envelope in which he had put a note telling Barbara to meet him in an hour at the grocery store she frequented.

He told the boy he'd give him another five bucks if he came back with proof he delivered the message. The boy came back a short time later and Jeff gave him the money. Then he walked back to his car and drove to the store, where he waited for his sister.

She was there an hour later. Grabbing a cart, she began shopping. He took his own buggy and waited until she stood in front of the vegetables. "These apples don't look too fresh, don't they," he said, standing beside her.

Startled, she turned and looked at him. He smiled. "Don't act surprised, Barb. Stay calm. It's me…Jeff. I'm in disguise."

She picked up one of the apples. "I want to give you a hug, big brother, but I guess I'd better not."

"Good girl. You never know who's watching you. I don't want to linger too long. I need to talk to Maxine. Phone her and tell her I called. Don't tell her you saw me. Ask her to come to your house tomorrow night. Invite her for supper. Tell her I want to meet with her Monday night at eight in the Acres Ranch Club, but don't say that on the phone. She knows where the place is. Okay?"

"Okay. Be careful. One more thing…Michael's boss phoned and told me he found something I might be interested in. He didn't tell me what. He asked me to pick it up, but I haven't gone there yet."

"I'll pick it up. Take care." He left without looking back and drove home. After spending the day watching TV and reading the newspaper, he decided to go to a movie theater. Sitting by himself in the theatre, he felt stupid and out of place. This was the first time in many years he'd actually gone to a movie. When Nicole was alive, they had been avid moviegoers, hardly missing the newest blockbusters.

Being alone just wasn't the same.

After the movie, he went to a bar and drank a couple of beers, alone and feeling sorry for himself. When a beautiful woman approached him and asked if he needed company, he declined, as tempting as it seemed.

"Your loss," she said, smiling. "A handsome hunk like you. I might even give it to you for free."

"Maybe I'm gay," he told her.

"Too bad." She walked away, looking for another mark.

Saturday nights can be such a drag. Even more so when you're alone.

Back home again, he turned on the television to watch the late night news. Staring at the screen with little interest, he sat up, suddenly wide-awake, when he saw a familiar face on the screen behind the news reporter.

Connie.

What the hell!

"Before we go to local news, we have a special report from our sister station in Fresno." The announcer looked at the small screen behind her. As the image grew, so did Connie's face for a moment. Then the camera switched to another reporter.

"Our guest tonight is Miss Connie Wu," the reporter said. "We've had a rash of murders lately in Fresno. Miss Wu's friend Dennis Kim was one of the murder victims. According to police reports, Mr. Kim was badly beaten in a botched robbery, but Miss Wu has a different theory. Can you please explain to our viewers what your thoughts are on this case?"

"For one thing," Connie said, "I don't believe Dennis was the victim of a botched robbery. The beating he received left him in a coma. He was admitted to hospital, where he was subsequently shot to death in the middle of the night. In his hospital bed. What reason would a robber have to murder him after he failed to rob him?"

She looked into the camera, her eyes and expression challenging the viewers.

"Maybe whoever tried to rob him was afraid Mr. Kim might identify him?" the reporter suggested.

"That's what the police seem to think. I don't believe that. His attackers wanted to kill him the first time. It was not a botched robbery but a botched murder attempt."

"Strong words, Miss Wu." The reporter smiled as the camera zoomed in on his face. "There are rumors that Mr. Kim was a homosexual. Is there any truth to those rumors?"

"Yes, the rumors are true."

"Perhaps it was a gay bashing?"

Connie's face filled the screen. Jeff had to admit, even in her obviously distressed condition, she looked beautiful. "So he was a homosexual! To murder him for that would have been awful. To kill another human being because of what he believes or because his lifestyle is not acceptable to some, is a terrible crime. However, Dennis was not the victim of a gay bashing. His death was not accidental, it was an execution."

"What makes you think that?"

"He was shot from close range behind the ear with a 9mm pistol. The pistol was equipped with a silencer."

"How do you know this, Miss Wu?"

"Apparently, nobody heard the shot. Had the killer not used a silencer, somebody would have heard something. As far as the caliber of the gun goes, I can't divulge my source."

"A friend in the police department?"

"No comment."

"I understand." The interviewer smiled. "After all, this is not an inquisition, just an in-depth look into one of the murders that happened nearly to the day two months ago. Do you have any theories why your friend was murdered, Miss Wu?"

"I have but I would prefer if you didn't ask me to elaborate. Not today, because I'm still collecting information. Perhaps next time I can tell you more."

"Thank you for your time and your candor, Miss Wu."

The picture faded and the local announcer came back on. Shuffling some papers, she smiled mechanically. "And now to local news..."

Jeff turned off the television set. He had misgivings about that interview. Appearing on TV would draw attention to Connie. People would take notice. The wrong people.

In the morning, he awoke to hear the sound of church bells in the distance and he felt like going to church. That was another thing he hadn't done for years.

Nicole had been the religious one. He had only gone along to keep her company.

People who are religious are lucky. At least they have hope to cling to, as faint as it may be. They have a place to go to on Sunday where they can reflect and even find peace. I've never felt that inside a church. Always felt out of place, like a character in a play. It always seemed unreal seeing people kneeling and praying to a god who probably only existed in their minds. A god who never answered their prayers. He certainly never answered mine.

Chapter Fifteen

When Jeff parked his rental car in front of Michael's old shop, Brent Cockburn, one of the mechanics, came out to see who it was.

"Can I help you?" he asked.

Jeff smiled, realizing that Cockburn didn't recognize him. "Is Bill Tucker in?"

"The boss? Sure, he's in. He might be busy though. Can I ask who you are? Your voice sounds familiar, but I can't place the face."

"I'm Jeff Chartrand, Michael's brother." Jeff grinned. "This red beard fools a lot of people."

Cockburn stared at Jeff and then he smiled. "You sure fooled me." He held out a hand. "I'd like to congratulate you for shooting that bastard Galliano. He deserved it. And so did Moretti. I had a run-in with him a while ago. Threw me out of the casino because I had a winning streak. Son of a bitch. That's what he was. Said I was cheating."

"Well, there are some people who don't support what I did."

"I know." He squinted against the sun. "I saw your picture all over the place. I guess they found you innocent?"

"Unfortunately, no. Not yet. About your boss? Can I talk to him?"

"Sure, sure. Come with me. He'll want to see you. By the way, thanks again for all the stuff you let us have. Michael sure had some expensive tools. He took care of them, too." The big man walked ahead of Jeff, held the door open for him.

Bill Tucker looked up from his desk when he saw Cockburn walking through the door. "What is it, Brent?"

"I brought a visitor, Boss."

Tucker seemed a little irritated. "I'm busy, Brent. When are you guys ever going to learn to announce someone before you bring them to the office?"

"Sorry, Boss, but this is Jeff, Michael's brother." He grinned when

140

Tucker stared at Jeff.

"Well, I'll be..." Tucker got out of his chair. "Chartrand. In disguise. You look like a goddamn doctor or something." He came around his desk and shook Jeff's hand. "I phoned your sister. I guess you spoke to her?"

"I have. She said you found something."

"Those goddamn sonsa bitches from Homeland Security. Came into my shop, tore things apart. Asked all kinds of stupid questions. Then they confiscated Michael's computer. Still haven't brought it back."

"Did they say what they were looking for?"

"No, but whatever it was, I don't believe they found it. I checked out Michael's computer myself and I noticed that some of his files were password protected. They even took his personal files from the filing cabinet, but they didn't get this." He walked back to his desk and pulled a small envelope from his desk drawer.

"There is a flash drive in there. He had it stuck into one of the files. I took it out before those guys came here. I want you to have it. Maybe it will help."

"Thanks, Mr. Tucker. I appreciate this."

"Call me Bill. Nobody calls me by my last name." He chuckled. "I don't like the way it sounds. I suffered enough as a kid when they purposely mispronounced my name. Kids can be cruel, you know."

"I guess they can be. Thanks again, Bill. I'll let you know if this helped me."

"Nail those bastards who murdered Michael. He was a good guy."

Jeff drove away with mixed feelings. Those guys from Homeland Security just didn't give up trying to find dirt on him and on Michael. He didn't believe for one minute that they were interested in finding the murderers.

He stopped for lunch in the same café Rob took him for breakfast. The waitress recognized him and gave him a bright smile. "Hi. Where is your friend?"

"My friend?" Jeff shrugged. "Busy, I guess. How's your friend?"

"Mine? Oh, you mean my boyfriend. We broke up."

"He's an idiot. How can anyone break up with a beautiful girl like you?"

She laughed. "You're a charmer, but you're right, he was an idiot.

He suffered from roaming hands, if you know what I mean."

"I know. Some guys are like that." He remembered his own youth. Remembered his own roaming hands. It's not easy for a guy to keep his hands away from a beautiful girl, especially for a guy with raging hormones.

"What can I get you?"

"What do your recommend?"

"Well." She leaned closer. He could smell her perfume as she hovered beside him, looking at the menu. "We don't have much to offer, but I recommend the fries and the chicken fingers. You can't go wrong there. We have a great lemon pie for desert. You'll love it."

"Okay. You convinced me." He inhaled the faint aroma of her feminine body, thinking of Connie. She was slim and graceful like this girl but older and more mature. Closer to his age, anyway.

Before she walked away, she brushed his shoulder with her hand, as if by accident. He felt a sudden fluttering in his loins.

She's too damn young, you fool.

He could almost hear Nicole's voice speaking to him. As much as he loved Connie and as much as he cared for Maxine or Kalila, Nicole would forever be the one dearest to his heart. Her memory would always keep him from making a mistake.

When the girl brought his food, she put it down in front of him with a smile. "Enjoy," she told him. Then she whispered, "I'm free tonight. Here is my phone number. My name is Julia." She shoved a small piece of paper under his plate.

Damn! It would be tempting to take her up on her invitation, but he knew it would be a stupid thing to do. The last thing he needed was to get involved with a young girl. She didn't look older than nineteen. She might be twenty, but no older than that.

Besides, she felt lonely because her boyfriend left her. Right now, she was on the rebound. *Girls in that state of mind can be quite hot because they want to prove they have what it takes to keep a man attracted to them. Maybe I should accept her offer. I have nothing to lose.*

He ate his chicken fingers, and he had to admit, they were good. *Soft and juicy. As soft and juicy as Julia would be.*

She brought him his coffee and the lemon pie. "It's the end of my shift," she whispered. "Call me, okay?"

He watched her walking away, hips swinging. *It would sure be easy to get into her pants. That girl is available.*

He smiled, finishing his coffee. *Looks like I still have it. Maybe it's the red beard.*

Of course, he had no intentions phoning her. He had a date with Maxine. He could not miss that.

He spent the afternoon in the gym and had a good workout. After a shower, he dressed, defrosted a frozen dinner, and drank a beer. He left the building shortly before seven. The place he had in mind was almost an hour's drive away, depending on traffic.

One thing with the place he picked, there were always many people there and he wouldn't be too obvious sitting by the bar. He chose a stool close to the corner, which allowed him to watch the entrance to the place.

He spotted Maxine the moment she walked into the room. Looking around, her eyes locked with his and she threaded her way through the people on the dance floor. She slid onto the empty chair beside him but didn't look at him. "Gin and Tonic," she told the bartender. Then she said, "Do you come here often?"

Jeff chuckled. "How did you know it was me?"

"Barbara described you in detail. That red hair and your beard. Not exactly a good way to blend into a crowd."

"Well, so far it's kept me out of trouble. How have you been?"

"Better. You should come in and give yourself up. It might make things easier. You still have friends in the Department."

"Are you one of them, Maxine?"

"Don't insult me. You know I am." Her eyes met his in the mirror behind the bar.

"It doesn't matter. I have to stay free." He wanted to turn and take her into his arms, kiss her soft mouth. She looked so attractive in her white outfit.

"How did you get out?"

"Long story. There is no time to tell you now. Did you find out anything new?"

She took a sip from her glass and turned her head. "Yes, I did. Something very interesting. I've been digging around in Galliano's files and I discovered he was the second cousin of a man by the name of Anthony Mariano, who happens to be the Godfather of the Chicago mob."

"I know who he is. This is quite some coincidence. You might find this intriguing. Somebody told me the same thing a few days ago."

She blew air across her lips. "I haven't told you everything I found out. It gets even more curious. It is no secret that Galliano and the DA were friends. Actually, they were more than just friends. The DA's wife and Galliano were first cousins."

She waited for a moment, nursing her drink. When he didn't answer, she said, "Did you get that?"

"Oh, I got it all right. I don't know what to make of it. This is beginning to get complicated, but somehow the dots can be joined together. I have a friend who is very good a deciphering these types of puzzles. I'm going to give him this information." Jeff finished his beer. He stared at her in the mirror. "I've missed you, Maxine."

Her hand stole close to his, but didn't touch him. "I've missed you, too. I worried what might have happened to you. When I got in touch with the precinct that held you, they told me the Military took you into custody. When I made inquiries, I couldn't find out anything. You seemed to have vanished. People in the Military are certainly tightlipped."

"Have you had contact with Homeland Security?"

"I spoke to this MacKay once. He asked me about our relationship."

"What did you tell him?" He was curious to hear her answer.

"There is nothing to tell. We were partners, what else could I tell him?" Her eyes challenged him.

Somehow he was disappointed. Partners? Is that all we were? What about the night we spent together? Had it not been for the unfortunate incident with Ethan Grey our relationship might have grown into something more than just one intimate encounter. He shrugged. Sometimes things don't turn out. "Did you make sure you weren't followed?"

"Never gave it a second thought. Do you think I'm being watched?"

"Yes, I do. I know how these guys work. I'd better be going."

"I thought we might dance." Her invitation took him by surprise and he almost accepted. Almost.

He shook his head. "Too dangerous. Meet me tomorrow night at the 'Five Star Heaven Motel'. I'll be there by eight. Have another Gin and Tonic and give me a chance to drive away before you leave."

He got up and walked briskly out of the room. He had been watching the entrance and he was certain t nobody tailed Maxine. Maybe he was just too damn paranoid, but he couldn't shake the feeling he might be running out of time. He couldn't become complacent and relax. Usually, when you felt most secure, that's when disaster struck

If anyone had somehow managed to come in undetected, the noise in the room would have drowned out Maxine's and his conversation. Even the latest surveying hardware would not be able to listen in. He was confident of that. But then he couldn't be certain. He saw what Rob had been able to accomplish.

He needed to get the information Maxine gave him to Detective Smith, but first he needed to talk to Rob.

Driving home, he found himself checking the rear view mirror, but when he arrived back at the warehouse, he didn't think anyone followed him. Before he went to bed he watched the late night news, but there was nothing interesting except for the usual muggings and break-ins.

Rob dropped in the next morning. Jeff told him about his meeting with Smith and with Maxine. Then he gave him Michael's flash drive and the envelope Connie had given him.

"I also found out a few things," Rob told him. "Those e-mails on Black's computer? They all originated in Chicago. Seems we have more than one reason to fly to Chicago. We need to find out who sent those orders to the 'Private Guards and Protection Agency' in Dallas. Maybe you and I can already connect some of the dots in the puzzle. We'll see what we find out. The more information we can gather the easier it will be for your detective friend to decipher it. If he's as good as you say."

He lifted the envelope. "What do you suggest I do with this?"

"Connie promised McGee she wouldn't open it until his demise. In a way, she broke that promise when she gave this envelope to me. Let's wait until we come back from Chicago then we'll see if we need to break her promise."

"What about this flash drive? No promise was made there?"

"No. Find out what's on it. Homeland Security took away my brother's computer. His files were password protected. Maybe this flash drive is also encrypted. See if you can break the code."

"Okay. Want to go for lunch?"

"Sure, but let's not go back to that café."

Rob threw him a puzzled look. "You didn't like the food?"

Jeff chuckled. "Oh, I liked the food all right. I liked more than that. Let's say I want to avoid temptation."

"Whatever." Rob shook his head. "You're talking in riddles, my friend. I know another fine place that serves delicious food. I'll take you there in my car. It's cheaper on gas than your rented clunker."

"By the way, how was Washington?"

Rob smiled mysteriously. "You think you're the only one who discovered a few things? Well, let me tell you about Colonel O'Connor. A reliable source tells me that he has shares in one of the companies that supply the Military with weapons."

"I don't know what we can do with that information. He's doing nothing wrong. I'm sure many Americans have shares in those companies."

"Not as many as he has. He is a major shareholder. I've investigated that company and, apparently, there are discrepancies with orders and deliveries. I haven't had enough time to do a thorough check. But it raises a flag."

* * * *

Maxine walked into the lobby of the motel at exactly eight o'clock. She looked stunning it her short white skirt that showed off her tanned long legs.

He watched her from his place on the couch as she approached him, a little smile on her face.

"Found you," she said.

He rose and gave her a quick kiss on the lips. "I've reserved a room," he said.

She raised an eyebrow. "Aren't you taking things for granted?"

"I am." He put his arm around her waist. She leaned into him as they walked toward the elevator.

Another couple entered the elevator ahead of them, a young man and woman, chattering about some show they had seen. Jeff and Maxine stayed silent. They stepped out of the elevator on the third floor and walked down the carpeted corridor. Once the door of the room closed behind them, Maxine was in his arms and kissed him feverishly. She fairly ripped off his shirt and opened his belt.

"Hurry," she breathed. "I can hardly wait. I've thought about you all day."

When he was naked, she got on her knees in front of him and caressed his penis with her lips. He groaned when she began teasing him with her tongue.

He took her face between his hands and pulled her up. "I don't want to come like that," he murmured. Then he smiled. "I like my women nude."

She stepped out of her skirt, her blue eyes watching him, and removed her thin blouse, exposing her breasts. A tiny thong covered her pubis, and when she turned, she displayed her full naked buttocks.

"You took a chance walking around like that with that short skirt of yours," he said, admiring the shape of her posterior.

She laughed. "Some girls don't wear anything at all under their skirts." She put her hands against his chest and pushed him toward the bed. "Sit down."

He sat on the edge and waited for her to come to him. Turning around, she presented her shapely backside to his view. She lifted up and slid her moist sheath over his hard organ. Holding on to her breasts, he just sat and watched her buttocks moving in his lap.

"This feels good," she moaned. "You feel good. I needed this."

Afterwards, when they lay on the bed in each other's arms, she snuggled up against him. "You never told where you were all this time."

"I was in Iraq." There was no reason to lie to her. He knew he could trust her.

"Does this mean you are back in the Military?"

"I never really left. Remember when I told you about what I did before I was discharged?"

"You told me you were in Army Intelligence, but you never told me exactly what you did."

"We did things that needed to be done. Some of them best forgotten."

She twisted in his embrace and looked into his face. "We've been partners for a number of years, but you never spoke about your time in the army. Was what you did so bad?"

He chuckled. "Everyone wants to live a good life. A life without crime and worries. Everyone wants to be free. There are people out there who are willing to take away this freedom. They are hungry for power and they will stop at nothing to achieve and maintain this power. Then there are people who desire money. People without scruples who will do anything to get what they desire, including selling out their country. And then there are people who are willing to stop them."

"Are you one of those people?"

"The ones looking for power or money?"

"No. The ones who are willing to stop them."

He could feel her soft breasts against his chest, felt the beating of her heart, the warmth of her body. It was good to hold her. Her eyes were still searching his face.

"Yes, I am," he said softly. "But it comes with a price."

"Your job in Iraq? Did you accomplish what you set out to do?"

"I believe I did. We did. However, it never ends. As one of the men in my unit pointed out, it's like taking out a drug dealer. Soon another one will take his place."

"How does Michael's murder fit into all of this?"

"I don't know. Not yet, but one thing I know, this was not a drug deal gone wrong. It has something to do with what happened when he was in Iraq."

"What about Galliano?"

"He was part of it, I'm certain. He was involved in more than just gambling and drugs." His hand touched her back, came to rest on her buttocks. "Your butt's getting cold," he said, smiling.

"We could cover up." She rolled away from him and pulled the covers from under him and covered their bodies with it. "I don't know why they always make it so cold in these hotel rooms." She laughed. "Don't they know what goes on in them?"

His thoughts drifted to his time in Iraq. "It would have been nice to have some of this cool air in Iraq."

"I've never been in that part of the world. Does it get very hot there?"

His laughter exploded out of him. "How much do you actually know about Iraq, Iran, Afghanistan, or any of the other countries in the region?"

She shrugged. "Not much. To be honest, nothing."

"Why not?"

"I was never interested?"

"You and the majority of Americans. How many know the history of their country? Of other countries? You'd be amazed how many Americans know very little about Canada, our neighbor to the north. They think Canada is always covered by a blanket of snow."

"Isn't it?"

"I sincerely hope you're just teasing me now." He didn't laugh when he said it. "I've made it a point to study the Middle East. Out of necessity, I admit. There is so much history there, ours pales in comparison. You'd think those people should be more advanced than we are, but that, of course, is not the case. In many ways, they are quite backward. Most people are poor. They are held back by ruthless fanatics who want to rule them."

"You're telling me that they are backward because of their religion? Because they are Muslims?"

"No. Being Muslim has nothing to do with that. We have plenty of Muslims living in the Western World who have adopted modern living. The fault lies with their leaders and their clergy. Saddam Hussein was one of those leaders. He's gone, but there are plenty of others who would like to step into his shoes. Remember what I said about power? It is always about power. Iran used to be a modern country until the Shah was ousted in the Iranian Revolution in 1979 and the country was thrown back into the Middle Ages."

She chuckled and stroked his chest. "I never knew you were such a philosopher."

"There is much you don't know about me." He thought about Connie. He loved her, and yet, here he was in the arms of another woman he was fond of, possibly also loved.

"Not all Muslims are bad," he said, remembering Kalia. She had bewitched him. He wanted nothing more than have sex with her; it would have been easy to fall in love with her. "Not all of them are our enemies. Not every Iraqi hates us, even though it is true the majority of Iraqis wants us out of their country. We invaded them without just cause."

"You really believe that?" She gave him an astonished look. "Many

Americans would dispute that and call you a traitor."

He sighed. "They would. They don't know that I am more of a patriot than many of those who would accuse me. Propaganda can twist a man's mind and make him blind to the truth, here in America, in Iraq or any other country."

"You're right, Jeff, you do talk like someone I don't really know. Have you always felt this way?"

"No, but sometimes things happen and you begin to wonder and ask questions. You begin to see the world with different eyes. However, I'm an American and I will always defend my country against an enemy who wants to take away my way of life. That will never change."

"I'm glad to hear that." She moved on top of him and kissed him. "Now shut up and make love to me."

"Again?"

"That's right, again. Prepare yourself for a long night. I'm just getting started."

Chapter Sixteen

Rob came to visit Jeff in the morning. Jeff didn't recognize him when he walked into the room and drew the gun he carried in his belt behind his back. He carried the gun just as a precaution, he told himself. Not because he was becoming paranoid.

"Whoa, whoa, don't shoot! It's me…Rob."

Jeff put down the gun. "What the hell, Rob? Don't walk in here looking like that!"

Rob laughed. "I guess my new disguise passed the test. Even you didn't recognize me."

Jeff stared at the young man's face. He had dyed his hair blond. A thick, bushy mustache adorned his upper lip. The twirled ends lend him a bit of an old-fashioned look.

"What's with those rings in your ears?" Jeff asked. "If it weren't for that ugly mustache you'd look like a girl."

"I gather you don't care for earrings?"

"Not unless they're worn by a girl or woman. As far as I'm concerned, a guy with an earring looks like a sissy." Jeff snorted disgustedly. "Only fags wear them."

Rob chuckled. "Well, I'm not a fag. I like women. And you, my old-fashioned friend, had better join the twenty-first century. Like it or not, men are wearing jewelry in their ears."

Jeff snorted again. "Maybe they should pull one through their nose while they're at it. This is not a new thing. Primitives wear them in the jungle. Pirates used to wear huge earrings, but that doesn't mean it made them into mucho men. A lot of sailors in those days were homosexuals."

"Who says that?"

Jeff shrugged. "So I've heard."

"How about men and ponytails?"

"Don't like them either. Especially on old men."

"Why am I not surprised?" Rob grinned and opened the gym bag he'd been carrying. He pulled out an object and threw it at Jeff, who caught it before it hit the floor.

Jeff looked at it. "Looks like hair. What do you want me to do with this?"

"Put it on your head. It's a wig. Time to change your disguise."

Jeff pulled the hairpiece out of the plastic bag and unfolded it. "At least it's not red," he said. Then he cursed. "Come on, Rob. A ponytail? I'm not wearing this."

"It's the perfect disguise." Rob threw something else onto the table.

A passport.

Jeff opened it and looked at the picture inside. It showed a man sprouting a dark blond mustache and a narrow strip of beard running down on each side of his bare chin. "I notice my name is Jerry Hammer."

"It's a good name."

"Why the change anyway?"

"One can never be too careful. You should know that." Rob produced a barber kit and some dye. "And now, let me transform you."

"I'm not wearing an earring!"

Rob sighed. "I thought it might be a good touch, but it is not a requirement of your new persona."

* * * *

They left for Chicago the next day. Rob came in a taxi and picked up Jeff. Then they drove to the airport. Jeff had to get used to being called 'Mr. Hammer'. Even though boarding the plane didn't cause them any trouble, he was happy to be sitting in his seat. Rob brought a book and Jeff was content with just sitting and relaxing. He hadn't done much of that lately.

After arriving in Chicago they checked into their hotel and spend the evening relaxing. Early next morning, they took a taxi to the nearest rental car agency and rented a car.

They found the address Rob had written in the small journal he carried in his pocket. It turned out to be the place of an export company. Moore's Exotic Exports. When they stepped into the office, they discovered it consisted of one room with two desks. One of them was occupied by a young girl.

She looked up when they entered. "Can I help you?"

She had a pleasant voice and face, black lips and overly long black eye lashes, with blue lids. Jeff noticed she was somewhat on the chubby side. The dress she wore seemed a bit too tight around her ample breasts, which she displayed quite freely.

"Are you alone in this place?" Rob asked.

His question made her look at him, sudden fear in her eyes. "No, I'm not alone."

"I don't see anyone else."

"My boss should be back any moment." Her voice sounded almost hysterical.

"We're not here to hurt you," Jeff said soothingly. "We just want some information. Since you're the only one here, we hope you can help us."

"What kind of information?"

"You sent a number of e-mails to a private recruitment agency in Dallas."

"I don't remember sending any e-mails to anyone in Dallas."

"Lying to a Federal Officer is a criminal offence!" Rob spoke sharply. "We know those e-mails originated here. All we have to do is check your hard drive."

"You'll find nothing on my computer," she said defiantly.

Rob's smile chilled even Jeff. He had to admit, Rob had talent. He should have been an actor. "That's what you think. Even if you deleted them, they're still there. All of them. Once written onto a hard drive information stays there forever or until you smash it into tiny pieces. And even then we'd be able to retrieve the information."

"I didn't know that." Her voice sounded small, scared.

"Well, don't feel too bad. Not many do." He allowed himself a tiny chuckle. "Something else people don't know is that home computers and the Internet are in fact a government conspiracy. The government's goal is to have a computer in every home."

"Why?"

"So the government can snoop on its citizens. The Internet is a wonderful medium and so are e-mails. They are the best in a way because they are not only stored in your own computer or the recipient's but also on your server's computer. Usually, for many years. Do you have a camera on your monitor?"

"Not here but I have one on my home computer?"

Rob nodded as if pondering something important. He lifted a finger, like a lecturer. "Cameras are another brilliant invention. You ever send naked pictures of yourself to your boyfriend?"

She blushed. "No, of course not."

"Lucky then for you, because all pictures are intercepted and stored on a special file the government is compiling on every citizen. Just in case they are needed at some later date."

"How do you know all this?"

"Because we are representing the government. We know everything." Rob pulled a wallet out of his inside jacket pocket and flipped it open. "Special Agent Roberts. That's me, and my partner here is Jerry Hammer."

"FBI?" the girl asked, clearly frightened and intimidated. "I admit, I've sent e-mails to Dallas, but I only forwarded them. It's just a game. I didn't think I was committing a crime."

"A game? What kind of game?"

She shrugged. "I don't know. Some kind of war game."

"Who's playing it?"

"My boyfriend."

"Does this boyfriend have a name?"

"His name is Jimmy. Jimmy Marco."

"Where can we find him?"

She hesitated. "Are you going to arrest him? I mean…he's just playing a game. Anyway, that's what he told me. Isn't he?"

"We only want to talk to him," Rob assured her. "For is own protection. He might have gotten himself involved in something that could be dangerous to his health…if you know what I mean. Even his life could be endangered."

"What about me?" She looked at Rob and then at Jeff. "I've done nothing wrong."

Jeff gave her a friendly smile. "As long as you cooperate you have nothing to fear. We are not the bad guys."

"Thank you. He works for Nova Investments. I don't know the address."

Rob nodded, pulled out his little notebook and wrote something into it. "We'll find it. Don't you go now and warn him, okay? We'll know.

Remember…Big Brother is watching."

"I'll remember."

"By the way, just for the record. How do you spell your name?"

She spelled it slowly and Rob scribbled again in his notebook. "Thank you, Miss Lange."

After they left the building, Jeff said, "Big brother is watching, huh? You sure scared that girl. You almost made me believe it."

Rob grinned. "Maybe you should believe it. I didn't make up the stuff about the e-mails and about certain government agencies spying on web surfers through the Internet. They can trace any IP address. Nobody is safe. How do you think they find all those pedophiles?"

"I actually never gave it a second thought. I'm not really into the Internet."

"That doesn't surprise me, either. You are a dinosaur. A dying breed. These days everybody and his grandmother is wasting hours upon hours on the Internet, checking out what to feed their canary and where to buy the latest erotic novel. And that is the tame stuff."

"That remark about the pictures?"

Rob laughed. "I made that up. I thought it gave it a nice touch." He shrugged. "But then you never know. Maybe it is true."

Jeff smiled and shook his head. "I told you this once, Rob. You are a sick boy. At one time in the future you may have to seek professional help if you keep this up."

"Thank you for the compliment, Jeff. It means a lot to me."

"You're welcome."

"I didn't make up the stuff about the hard drive, though. Information can easily be retrieved, even if it has been deleted and 'shredded'."

Jeff sighed. "You called me a dinosaur and you may be right. I don't like this so-called computer age. There is no more privacy. Too much information is being broadcast. All these kids with their cell phones that take pictures, send text messages, and play games. Somebody does something stupid and the next day it is being watched by people all over the world."

"It's called progress. Actually, this is the information age."

"Call it what you will, I'm not a fan. I wouldn't be surprised if somebody somewhere is watching us right now over the satellite, wondering what we're up to."

"Don't go paranoid now on me, old man. Nobody knows we're here. Of course, if anyone interested would know about our whereabouts, they could track us."

"There you go. Don't tell me you are enthused about such a possibility?"

"I'm not, but every coin has two sides. If I'm the watcher then I have no problem with it. You saw what we did in Iraq."

"Yes, I remember, and I'm still amazed at what the Military is capable of."

"You have no idea." Rob changed lanes and said, "We should almost be there. I think it's that tall building ahead, the one with all the glass."

"You can tell who's making all the money. Investment and insurance companies," Jeff commented.

Rob didn't answer. He was too busy looking for a place to park. He found one not too far from the building when some other driver pulled out into the street to vacate a parking spot.

Getting into the building was easy, because the first floor was occupied by a series of small shops. The offices of the investment company were located on the ninth floor. They took the elevator and stepped into a plush foyer.

The receptionist behind the desk was busy doing her fingernails. She gave them a friendly smile. Jeff had to admit she did look much better than the girl from the import company. It was obvious this place hired their girls because of their looks and not necessarily because of their qualifications.

"We're looking for Mr. Marco," Rob said.

Her smile grew wider. "Oh, Jimmy. Yes, he's in. Do you have an appointment?"

"No, but he'll see us." Rob's smile matched hers.

"May I ask your name?"

"Mr. Roberts and Mr. Hammer."

"I'll see if he is free." She chuckled. "He should be. He doesn't get too many clients." She pressed a button on her phone. "A Mr. Roberts and Mr. Hammer to see you, Jimmy."

She looked up after a few moments.

"He'll see you. Please follow me."

She was tall, with a nice figure, and Jeff watched her plump buttocks as she walked in front of them, thinking of Maxine, wondering what she was doing at the moment.

Jimmy Marco turned out to be a skinny young man, not much older than Rob. When he rose from behind his desk, Jeff noted his height. He towered even over Jeff, who stood six feet and one inch. His dark curly hair was already receding from his high forehead. Jeff gave him five or six more years before he'd be bald.

He beamed at them. "What can I do you gentlemen for?"

His smile vanished when Rob flipped open his wallet and flashed his fake ID.

"FBI," Rob said with a crisp voice. "We are investigating a case of Internet fraud. You've sent e-mails to Miss Candy Lange at Moore's Exotic Exports. She forwarded those e-mails to Private Guards and Protection Agency in Dallas."

"Who told you that?" Marco sounded almost belligerent, but Jeff detected the edge of sudden fear.

Rob emitted an exaggerated sigh and turned to Jeff. "Do we have to repeat this whole drama we went through with Miss Lange, Mr. Hammer?"

Jeff smiled grimly, falling into the role of a mean government agent. "I believe we've wasted enough time with his girlfriend. I'd say we just arrest him and take him down to headquarters for interrogation. We have enough evidence to stuff his head and nail his hide against the wall."

"I agree, Mr. Hammer. Interrogating Miss Lange left me all jittery and nervous. Upset even. I only dislocated her arm, but interrogating Mr. Marco now might upset me even more. You know how I get. I might break his arm or do something else to him."

"Hey, listen you guys! You can't just come into my office and make threats. I have rights, you know. I'm calling my lawyer." Marco grabbed his phone.

Rob reached him with two strides and clamped his fingers over Marco's hand. "Not so fast, Mister. You call your lawyer when we say so. When dealing with the Federal Government you have very few rights." He spoke coldly. "I suggest you cooperate with us. Playing hardball will only be detrimental to your case."

Marco wiped his free hand across his perspiring forehead. "Your nails are digging into my hand."

Rob removed his hand and smiled almost jovially. "Jimmy, Jimmy. Come on, make it easy for yourself and us. It's been a long day and my partner and I are very tired and irritable. Help us and we'll go easy on you."

Marco rubbed his hand and went to sit in his chair. Reaching into a drawer, he pulled out a packet, removed a cigarette and pushed it between his lips. Then he lit it with trembling fingers. Blowing smoke through his nose, he sat silent for a moment. Then he said, "What do you want to know?"

"Your girlfriend told us you're playing some kind of war game, but we both know that is not true, Jimmy. We know you've been sending these e-mails to Dallas. Please don't insult us by denying it. We want to know who you are working for."

Marco looked puzzled. "I work for Nova Investments, but you know that."

"Are you telling us that Nova Investments is hiring mercenaries?" Jeff asked.

"Hiring mercenaries?" Again, that puzzled look.

"That's right. Don't pretend you don't know." Jeff looked at Rob. "Maybe you can help Mr. Marco to remember."

"There is nothing to remember," Marco protested. "I really don't know what you are talking about. I'm getting my orders from Mr. Hardini. He's my boss."

"From Mr. Hardini? Are you sure?"

"I'm sure."

Jeff glanced at Rob again. "I believe he is telling the truth. What do you think?"

Rob nodded. "It seems Mr. Marco is finally cooperating, but he obviously is not our man. He's just another innocent player, like Miss Lange. We should talk to Mr. Hardini."

Jeff stared at Marco. "If you've given us the correct information we won't press charges against you, Mr. Marco, but you're not entirely in the clear. You have, unknowingly it seems, taken part in a conspiracy against the United States of America. That is a serious offence. Depending how the rest of our investigation plays out, you might just walk away unscathed if you keep our conversation to yourself. Do you understand?"

Marco nodded eagerly. "I understand. I had no idea. I just followed orders."

"Better start thinking for yourself, Jimmy," Rob said in a friendly tone. "You're not in the army where you have to follow orders without asking questions. Next time make sure you are aware of what you're getting yourself into."

"I will. Thank you, sir."

"Oh, and one more thing. Smoking causes cancer, mainly of the lungs. You're already going bald. Do you want to add wheezing to that?"

"I haven't thought about that."

Rob winked and clucked. "Maybe you should take my advice and lay off that habit. You'll thank me later."

"Does your boss work in this office?" Jeff asked.

"Yes. I believe he's in, but you'll have to talk to Mindy, our secretary."

They left Marco's office, leaving behind a shaken young man. Jeff didn't doubt he told them the truth. He was usually a good judge of character. Jimmy Marco didn't have it in him to be involved in something as big as this. He was just an innocent pawn in a much larger game.

Mindy was still busy doing her nails, but she seemed all bubbly and eager to announce them to Mr. Hardini. "Just follow me. Again." She giggled and walked ahead of them down the carpeted corridor.

Jeff noticed Rob's eyes riveted on Mindy's nicely shaped buttocks and smiled, watching their play in her tight skirt. *I guess he's an assman, just like me. She does have a nice ass, though. Probably knows how to move it with great skill in a man's lap.*

"Here we are, gentlemen." Mindy knocked on the door with the sign 'Benny Hardini' on it. She opened it when a voice from inside called, "Come in."

"Mr. Hammer and Mr. Roberts, Mr. Hardini," she announced them.

"Thanks, Mindy."

"You're welcome, Mr. Hardini." She closed the door behind them.

The man behind the desk looked at them expectantly. "You've caught me at a bad time. I was just about to leave the office to meet with a client. What can I help you with?"

Rob went again through the ritual of flipping his fake badge. "You may just have to cancel that meeting, Mr. Hardini. We have reason to believe you are involved in treasonous activities," Rob said.

"What do you mean?"

Jeff saw the hostility in the man's eyes and knew he would not crack the way Marco had.

"You are hiring mercenaries to be used in acts that involve the illegal sale of arms to enemies of the United States of America." Rob got right down to the gist of it. Just like Jeff, he realized there was no reason to mince words with this man.

Hardini stared at them, and then he threw back his head and broke into loud laughter.

"You think that is funny?" Jeff asked.

Hardini wiped his eyes. "Yes, it is funny and totally absurd. Why would I want to do that, whatever it is you accused me of?"

"That's what we are trying to find out. Why would an obviously successful businessman like you get involved in criminal activities?" Rob asked, almost gently.

Hardini laughed again. "Who are you guys?"

"I guess you didn't get a good look at my ID," Rob said. "We are Federal Agents. We are members of a special branch that deals with threats to the country. And right now you seem to be part of those threats."

"I thought that was the job of the Department of Homeland Security."

Rob gave a short chuckle. It sounded almost like a snort. "Those guys pale against us. We can find out things they can't, mainly because they have to follow rules, we don't."

"Well, whatever it is you have found out about me, it isn't true. I sell insurance and investment opportunities. There is nothing illegal about that. You must have me confused with someone else."

"I don't believe so. We have sound information."

"Who gave you this sound information?" Hardini leaned back in his chair and gave Rob a challenging stare.

Jeff had been studying the man. He seemed of average height, well built. Probably worked out in a gym. Handsome with his dark looks. Sure of himself and his abilities. He would admit to nothing.

"Your employee Mr. Marco ratted you out, Mr. Hardini."

"I should have guessed. That punk is trying to get me into trouble. I got him off the street, gave him a nice, cushy job. God knows, he doesn't do much all day long. Just sits behind his desk playing computer games. He doesn't think I know about it." He threw up his hands. "You know what they say about doing someone a favor. Nobody ever thanks you for it. This is how he repays my kindness."

"Does this mean you are denying his accusation?"

"It most certainly does! This is so ridiculous I don't even know how to deal with it."

"Well, then there should be no problem. Just let us examine your computer and check out some of your files and we can clear up this problem in a short time." Rob smiled. He looked like an undertaker about to hand the bill to the grieving family.

Hardini's dark eyes stared at Rob, unflinching. Then his lips formed a tight smile. "I think you've overstayed your welcome, gentlemen. I suggest you remove your unwanted persons out of my office before I call my lawyer."

Rob chuckled. "Such formal language. Does this mean you won't let us take a look at your computer files?"

Hardini pointed at the door. "Out!"

"That's making it quite clear. How can we refuse such a polite request?"

"I have friends in high places."

"Doesn't everybody?" Rob looked at Jeff. "I guess we'll have to go and get a court order."

Jeff shrugged. "Seems that way. This also proves we are on the right track. What other reason to deny us access to the company's computer." He gave Hardini a hard look. "We'll be back and you'd better have a good explanation why you won't let us check out your files. Maybe you should arrange for someone to replace you while you're rotting in jail waiting for your trial. Cuba is quite hot this time of year."

"What has Cuba to do with this?"

"Didn't you know that's where all the enemies of the State are held? I hear the guards there still use old-fashioned interrogation tactics." Jeff allowed himself an evil chuckle. "Think about that until we come back." He glanced at Rob. "Let's go."

When they stood in the elevator, Rob grinned. "That went quite well, don't you think so?"

"We are no further in our investigation than we were when we came." Jeff shook his head. "We still don't know anything concrete."

"But we do. That Hardini is as guilty as sin. Too bad, though. Now he's been warned and he may clear his computer. We'll have to find a way to get at his hard drive. I'll be able to retrieve the information," Rob said, musing.

They stopped talking when the elevator doors opened and a couple of girls entered. Rob smiled at them. "Nice weather we're having," he said.

Both girls gave him a puzzled look. Then they turned away, ignoring the men.

Rob chuckled. "That's the trouble in these big cities. Nobody talks to a stranger anymore. Where I come from, we say 'hi' to everyone."

Jeff grinned. "Where you come from even the cows say 'hi' to you."

The girls giggled and looked at each other, shrugging. The elevator stopped again, taking on another rider. An older man. He nodded to Rob and Jeff but ignored the girls.

In their car, Jeff said, "Let's get back to our hotel room. I'd like to find out more about this Benny Hardini and I just know the man who can do it."

"Who?"

"My friend Marvin Smith."

"The detective?"

"That's him. He'll be more than anxious to help us out."

Chapter Seventeen

Jeff was lucky to catch Smith in his office. After listening to Jeff's request, Smith said, "It's Friday. I won't be able to have anything for you until Monday."

"That's fine. I'll call you back Monday."

Smith didn't ask why Jeff didn't leave a phone number.

Jeff and Rob slept in Saturday morning. Then they went for breakfast.

"Maybe we can find a gym," Rob suggested.

Jeff agreed. It wouldn't hurt to exercise.

They spent the morning in the gym. In the afternoon, they went sightseeing. Jeff felt like a tourist. He was anxious to get on with the job, but there was no sense rushing it. They had to wait until Monday. He bought a book in one of the bookstores in case he became bored.

In the evening, they went to a bar, where Rob picked up a woman. Jeff went back to their room and started reading his book.

Rob didn't come home until late in the morning. Jeff woke up when he heard the water rushing.

"I'm going to spend some time with the young lady I picked up last night," Rob announced at breakfast.

"In other words you'll be leaving me alone," Jeff said.

"That's right, Amigo," Rob grinned.

"Amigo?" Jeff lifted an eyebrow. "I didn't know we were in Mexico."

"The young lady I met is Latino." He grinned and shook one hand. "She's hotter than red chili peppers on a taco."

"Just make sure you don't get burned, Compañero," Jeff said.

After breakfast, Jeff went back to the gym. Rob was gone for the rest of the day and the evening. He walked into the hotel room just before midnight.

"I didn't expect you yet," Jeff said. "What happened? Ran out of Salsa?"

Rob grinned. "No, sir. Everything you can imagine happened, but she has to go back to work in the morning. Needs to rest up."

When Jeff phoned Smith the next morning, Smith did have the information he was seeking.

"I found out that this Benny Hardini has a brother, Terrence Hardini, who works for Anthony Mariano." Smith paused to let Jeff absorb the information. "That's right. The Godfather. Anthony Mariano is the owner of *Banco Mariano*, one of the large private lending institutions." He paused again. "Be warned, Jeff. That's a nasty bunch. Mariano is a powerful man. He has connections all over the country and beyond. He's got politicians in his pocket, right up to the chief of police and even the mayor's office. Only rumors, but you know what they say. Where there is smoke there is fire. Be careful."

"I will. Thanks, Marvin. You've been a tremendous help. I'll keep you informed."

He hung up and told Rob about the news.

Rob whistled softly. "Wow, this is beginning to get interesting. I think we're finally getting somewhere. Now more than ever we need to get back into that office."

"I'd like to visit Mariano first. Maybe we can skip breaking into Hardini's office. We might just find out some stuff from the Godfather himself."

Rob grinned. "I like it. Right into the lion's den. There is no stopping us now."

"Don't be so enthusiastic, my young impatient friend. This lion might just decide to roar and make a meal out of us."

"We'll just roar back. Remember, we're not a couple of tame pussycats." Rob laughed. "I suggest we'll pretend to be two bad guys from Sacramento. Not FBI this time. It won't get us anywhere."

"What do you have in mind?" Jeff was always open to Rob's ideas. The young man was a genius when it came to inventing disguises and playing different roles. He would let him take the lead.

"You and I are cousins, two ambitious cousins, ready to take over the Sacramento mob. We came to ask for the Godfather's blessing."

"Sounds good. Let's hope he buys it."

"Don't sound so skeptical. We'll wing it. Let me handle the details. I'll come up with something." Rob pulled out his pen and notebook. "This is the stuff good novels are made of."

Jeff chuckled. "I forgot you're a writer. How is the novel going?"

"Good. I had to put it on hold for a while. Right now I'm just gathering information."

"Suffering from writer's block?"

"No. Like I said, I'm in the information gathering stage. Writing a novel involves much more than just sitting behind a typewriter or at a keyboard and moving your fingers. It involves a lot of research." Rob stared into space. "Right now I have to concentrate on the task at hand. Give me a few moments to myself."

"All right. How about we leave right after lunch. Mariano should be in his office then."

They drove away from their hotel at exactly one o'clock. It would take them over an hour to get to the Banco Mariano building.

Traffic was heavy, as usual, but Rob managed to weave his way through the congestion of cars. Jeff was happy Rob did the driving.

The building had a large underground parking lot. At least parking didn't present any problems.

When they stopped at the information desk and asked about Mariano, they were told that Mr. Mariano did not talk to anyone unless they made an appointment in advance. "He's a busy and important man," the young man behind the desk said. He had painted lips and eyes. A row of tiny diamonds adorned each of his ears.

"I'm sure he is." Rob gave him his big *innocent boy's* smile and touched the young man's hand in an intimate gesture. "It's just...we came all the way from Sacramento to talk to him. We are distant cousins, you know." He chuckled and rolled his eyes. "This city is so big and we had such a hard time finding this place. And this is such an awesome building. I had no idea Anthony is so important. It would be a shame if we didn't say at least 'hi'. My mother would be so disappointed." He turned to Jeff. "Right, Jeff, honey?"

The turn of events took Jeff by surprise and he wondered why Rob had suddenly developed a lisp. "Right, Rob...honey."

Rob giggled. "Jeff is so shy. He still pretends he isn't...you know. With being older and all that." He giggled again and rolled his eyes. "I love your make-up and I admire your courage to be so open."

"Oh, thank you." The man behind the desk rolled his eyes in turn. "You wouldn't believe how many people still give me these looks. They can be so mean."

Rob waved his hand. "I know exactly where you come from. What's your name?"

"Leslie."

"Hi, Leslie."

"Hi, yourself, Handsome. Let me see what I can do." Leslie wiped a strand of hair out of his face, picked up his phone and dialed a number.

Rob and Jeff waited patiently until Leslie was finished talking.

"You're in luck. I have a friend on Mr. Mariano's floor. He'll get you in to see him. He's on the fourteenth floor. Oh, one more thing. Take the public elevator to floor sixteen and use the stairs to get back down to fourteen. You want to avoid the body guards." He puckered his lips and smiled at Rob. "If you have some time maybe you and I can get together for a drink. Here is my number."

Rob pocketed the scribbled note. "Oh, that would be just fabulous. I'll try to make time. Thank you for everything, Leslie." He smiled and winked. "See you, Gorgeous."

Jeff waited until they were out of earshot. "What the hell was that all about…honey?"

Rob laughed. "Come on, Jeff. You must admit I was…ffffabulous."

Jeff couldn't keep himself from grinning. "You never cease to amaze me. You should be in the movies. I think you're wasting your abilities chasing bad guys."

"Oh, I know, but somebody has to chase the bad people, big guy. Did I ever tell you I love your gorgeous wide shoulders? Just looking at you makes me shiver all over."

"Don't overdue it now, Rob. You're making me feel uncomfortable."

Rob shrugged. "I'm a chameleon, my friend. I can adapt to any situation. It's a natural gift I was born with, like breathing."

"As long as you don't forget who you really are. You can stop the act now."

"You're just no fun." Rob sighed. Then he grinned. "Maybe it isn't an act. Maybe this is my real self. Would you still respect me if I told you I am gay?"

"Rob, for heaven's sake. Now you are really freaking me out. I have nothing against homosexuals, as long as they don't flaunt their sexual orientation in public and as long as they don't bother me. I don't care if you're gay or straight, as much as I care about the color of your skin. Be who you are and don't make a big deal out of it," Jeff said, becoming annoyed. "Now, can we get back to reality and concentrate on the job at hand?"

"We sure can. And don't worry, I'm as straight as they come and I will never hit on you again...honey."

Jeff shook his head and laughed. "You're incorrigible. That's why I love you."

"Now you're freaking me out, big guy."

They reached the elevators and waited for one to come down.

"This sure is a busy place," Jeff said, looking around. "And so plush. I'd almost be afraid to sit down in any of those chairs for fear of sinking away."

"It's a bank," Rob said. "You can tell by the way most of the customers are dressed that they're wealthy. They almost reek of money. And the tellers all wear suits. This place reminds me of an expensive restaurant with a maitre d' and only male waiters."

"Almost like one of those banks in Switzerland where people hide illegal money."

"You're probably hitting it right on the nail. Remember who owns this bank. There is more going on here than just banking, of that I'm certain," Rob agreed.

They stepped into the elevator and pushed the button for the sixteenth floor. Jeff noted that the building had twenty-four floors. Every floor belonged to Anthony Mariano. Either his bank generated all the money needed to run a huge building like this or he had other venues of revenue. Jeff had no doubt many of them included illegal activities.

"Well, here we are," Rob interrupted his thoughts. "Time to start playing our game."

Walking down the two flights of stairs, they didn't encounter anyone who could have stopped them. Only when they walked down the carpeted corridor, a young man suddenly stepped out of one of the rooms and blocked their way. He was gaudily dressed, with two rings in each ear. "Hurry," he said. "Follow me."

They were about halfway down the corridor when two burly men came out of another room. "Hey, where do you think you're going?" one of them asked.

Jeff saw the bulges under their jackets, but neither of the men made any threatening moves.

"Oh, hi, Anton. I'm taking my friends to see Mr. Mariano. They're relatives from the west coast," their escort told them.

"Relatives of Mr. Mariano? We were never told of any relatives visiting."

"It is a surprise visit," Jeff said. "A last minute thing because of the sudden death of a mutual friend. Anthony, I mean Mr. Mariano, was very close to him and we wanted to tell him in person."

"I don't know..." Anton eyed the young man. Then he looked at Rob who gave him a big smile.

"You've got big shoulders, big guy," Rob said, rolling is eyes.

Jeff cringed but kept silent, letting Rob take over.

The big man stared at Rob and shook his head. "Another one. There's more and more of them. Are you guys packing?"

"Packing?" Rob asked, rolling his eyes again. He looked down at his chest and then at his crotch. Giggling, he said, "Whatever you see is real."

"Do you have guns?"

Rob lifted both hands. "Guns? Are you kidding? Guns kill people."

"I'll have to frisk you anyway."

"Frisk me? That sounds dangerous." Rob giggled. "Sure, frisk me all you want."

"You do it," Anton told his partner. "I'll check the other guy."

Rob giggled again when the other man ran his hands along his sides. "Don't be afraid to touch me. I won't break. Did anyone ever tell you that you have strong but sensuous hands?"

"Oh, shut up, you freak," the man said, obviously annoyed. Jeff couldn't blame him. He felt like kicking Rob.

Anton frisked Jeff, but he wasn't very thorough. He never checked for an ankle holster. "Okay, go ahead."

"Thank you so much," Rob winked at Anton. "Maybe you and I..."

"It's never gonna happen, faggot." Anton glared at Rob and at the young man who stood smiling back at him. "I don't know why Mr. Mariano keeps you around, Jordan. Now, take your queer friends to Mr. Mariano and hope he's in a good mood."

"I'm not queer," Jeff said.

The man shook his head and sneered. "Who gives a fuck?"

Jeff felt like smashing his fist into the sneering face but kept his temper under control. He always hated guys like that. As a cop he hated them even more and it would have given him great pleasure to haul both these men to the next police station and book them for carrying concealed weapons. Most likely unregistered guns, he was certain of that.

He followed Jordan and Rob. They stopped in front of a door and were waiting for him to catch up.

Jordan knocked on the door. A moment later, it opened.

"Yes?" asked a woman's voice.

"Visitors for Mr. Mariano," Jordan said.

The young woman looked at Jeff and Rob. "Do you have an appointment? I don't remember anyone making one."

"We don't have one, but Mr. Mariano will see us. Tell him friends of Mr. Galliano from Sacramento want to talk to him."

"I'll tell him."

She closed the door, leaving Jeff and Rob waiting. It didn't take long before she came back.

Opening the door wide, she said, "Mr. Mariano will see you."

"Good luck," Jordan said, and then he rushed away.

Jeff and Rob followed the young woman into the room. It was a small office with a desk in the back and a few chairs against one wall. She led them to a door, opened it and told them to go right ahead.

The bright light streaming in through a huge window in the back of the room made Jeff squint for a moment. At first, he could only see the silhouette of someone sitting in front of the window behind a huge desk, but then his eyes adjusted and he was able to make out the features of the man.

He was big and fat, almost obese. Thinning, white hair covered his round skull. The huge glasses with the thick red frame gave him the appearance of a comical cartoon character out of a Disney movie, but one look into the eyes behind those glasses wiped out that impression.

He watched Jeff and Rob walking toward him and took the cigar he was smoking out of his mouth. Jeff expected to see thick lips to go with the rest of the round face but saw only a wide chin and a mouth like a knife.

The mouth didn't smile. "I agreed to see you because Jordan brought you, but make it fast. My time is valuable." He spoke with a rough, gravelly voice and wheezed like an ancient steam engine.

"So is ours, Mr. Mariano," Rob said beside Jeff. "Thank you for seeing us."

Mariano waved a hand. "Let's suspend with the formalities. What do you want?"

"We are from Sacramento. We were in the area and we thought we'd look you up, Mr. Mariano," Rob said smoothly.

"Why?"

"You remember Toni Moretti, Mr. Galliano's bodyguard?"

"Vaguely, but I know who you're talking about."

"Well, Toni was a good friend. Bless his soul. He was killed the day Mr. Galliano was shot by that renegade cop. The same son of a bitch shot Toni."

"You worked for Galliano?" Mariano puffed a blue cloud of smoke.

"Not actually worked for him. We did some contract work, that's all. We were at his funeral."

Mariano puffed more smoke. "I had to miss the funeral. Personal reasons. It would have been bad for my image to show up in Sacramento. I haven't kept up with the developments. Did they ever get that cop?"

"No. He disappeared."

"Too bad. What was his beef with Joseph anyway?"

"Seems he was the brother of a local war hero, who was eliminated, along with his family. He had the notion Mr. Galliano was behind the hit."

Mariano sat silent for a moment. He looked into the cloud of smoke he created around himself. "That whole thing was bad business." His glasses magnified his eyes. He fixed their gaze on Jeff. "You haven't said anything. Were you also one of Toni's friends?"

"I knew him but we were never friends." Jeff smiled. "I believe he was jealous of my special friendship with Joseph."

"You and Joseph were friends? What's your name?"

"Jeff Harper."

"He never mentioned your name."

"That's because I preferred to stay out of the limelight, Mr. Mariano, until now."

"What do you mean?"

"Joseph Galliano's job is still open. I want it."

"I thought Danny Leighton stepped in?"

Jeff gave a small laugh. "Leighton? That's not written in stone. He's not even Italian. Just because he's Galliano's brother-in-law means nothing."

"And you are Italian, Mr. Harper?"

Jeff didn't miss the sarcasm in Mariano's voice. "From my mother's side. Her maiden name was Selini."

"That means you're only half Italian."

"It seems that way at first, but that is not correct. I did some research and I discovered that my grandfather changed his name from Capone to Harper." Jeff allowed himself a smile. "I've always wondered why. I was thinking of changing it back to Capone."

Mariano actually laughed. "Interesting story. If true." He moved his big bulk in his chair. "Why did you really come? Just to chit-chat?"

"We wanted to meet you, Mr. Mariano. Now that Joseph Galliano is gone, somebody with ambition has to step in and carry on with the business."

"What business?"

"Well, you know…the business you had with Galliano."

"No, I don't know. I'm into banking not gambling. You tell me what business you're talking about."

"Can I talk freely?" Jeff looked around like someone about to reveal a deep secret.

"You can say anything you want in my office. It is not bugged. Nobody but me will hear it." Mariano's face disappeared momentarily behind a cloud of blue smoke.

"All right." Jeff lowered his voice. "Danny Leighton is weak. He will never be able to fill Galliano's shoes. Galliano didn't take him into his confidence. To tell the truth, he never trusted him fully."

"How do you know this?"

Jeff chuckled. "I make it my business to be informed. Joseph and I had long talks and I know more about the business than anyone. He told me about the hit on that Chartrand fellow. He also told me who gave the order."

"Who?"

Jeff mentally took a deep breath. This was the part that would decide what happened next. "You, sir. You did."

Mariano sat silent, just puffed on his cigar. Then he said, "What reason would I have to do that?"

Jeff shrugged. "He never told me and it didn't matter. Why did you?"

"You are treading on dangerous ground, Mr. Harper. If you want to do business with me, you do as Joseph did. You don't ask questions. Is that understood?" His voice carried a sudden edge.

"I understand. I know that you and I will never have the same relationship Joseph had with you. After all, he was your cousin. Family. I'm an outsider, but I think it can be to our mutual benefit if you make me part of your organization, Mr. Mariano." Jeff watched the fat man's face. He felt suddenly cold inside, knowing he was looking at the man who was responsible for Michael's death. He made himself a promise that he would revenge his brother's murder. He would make this man pay.

But not yet. He needed to know why Mariano, a mobster, would take out a hit on a man thousands of miles away. A man he didn't even know.

For the hundredth time he asked the same question.

What were you involved in, Michael? What caused someone like Mariano to order your execution?

He needed to find the answer. There would be time to come back to Mariano, time enough to blow out his brain.

Something in his expression must have betrayed his thoughts. Mariano gave him a long stare. "You look like a man who wants to put a gun to my head rather than someone who wants to join my organization." He laughed suddenly. "You must want it badly to be so intense. I hope you know what you're asking. It won't be a joyride. Only a strong man will be able to live up to my expectation. You won't be joining the boy scouts."

Jeff forced himself to smile. "I know that, Mr. Mariano. That's why

Danny Leighton is not the right man. I am."

"I must admit I like your confidence. Will you be long in town?"

"We'll probably fly home in a few of days."

"Where are you staying?"

Jeff hesitated. Would it be smart to tell him where? Especially since they were registered under different names. "We're staying at the Holiday Inn Chicago."

"Right downtown. I know where it is. How do you like Chicago?"

"I prefer Sacramento. Not as many people."

Mariano chuckled good-naturedly. "I like Chicago. I grew up here. It's my home. Lots of history and great opportunities for someone who likes to grab them. This is a beautiful city. Just look at the view." He pointed at the window.

Jeff stared at the jungle of tall buildings and had to admit it was breathtaking. If you liked buildings.

"That's my world out there." Mariano puffed on his cigar. "Do you smoke?"

"No. I'm a health nut." Jeff smiled.

"How about you?" Mariano looked at Rob.

Rob shook his head. "No, I like my lungs to stay clean. I plan to live a long time."

"Smoking isn't the only thing that kills people." Mariano smiled enigmatically. "Curiosity can be deadly. Remember that." He gave them a long look. "Come back in a couple of days, but this time make an appointment with my secretary. Get her number before you leave. Now, go."

"Thank you, Mr. Mariano."

They walked toward the door. Before they walked out, Jeff turned and said, "We'll be seeing you."

You bet your fat ass I will see you again. Next time I just might put a bullet between your eyes and end your miserable life, you wheezing walrus.

Chapter Eighteen

"That wasn't the smartest thing you did giving Mariano the name of our hotel. You should have given him a different address." Rob didn't sound happy.

"I thought about it, but I don't believe it would have made a difference. I gave him a false name."

"I know. Jeff Harper. What would have been wrong giving him your other false name?"

Jeff shrugged. "Because I am registered in the hotel under Jerry Hammer, that's why."

"I guess it doesn't matter." Rob looked into the rearview mirror. "I think we have a tail."

"What makes you say that?" Jeff checked the side mirror.

"That black Cadillac three cars behind us. I've been watching it. Every time I changed lanes that car did the same."

"Maybe just coincidence."

"I don't think so. I've spotted two guys in there, wearing suits and dark glasses."

"So are we."

"I know, but I have a pretty good eye for that. Believe me, those guys are following us."

"Can you lose them?"

"I don't know this city well enough to even try. They know it better than the two of us. Besides, they know where we're heading." Rob changed lanes again and chuckled. "Yep, they are following us. They're not even trying to be inconspicuous."

"Then let them. As long as they don't try to shoot at us. We can't even shoot back."

Rob snapped his right arm and suddenly he held a small gun in his hand. "We can if we have to."

174

"What the hell!" Jeff exclaimed, surprised.

Rob grinned. "You didn't think I'd go into a bullpen without a weapon?"

"*I* went without one."

"Did you forget the first things you learn in this business? *Don't trust anyone. Suspect everything and everyone. Don't become attached to anyone.*" Rob gave Jeff a sidelong glance.

"It's been a long time since I lived by that code. I tried hard to forget it and become a normal human being again."

"Have you succeeded?"

"I thought I had. Now I'm not so sure anymore." Jeff smiled. "You are not a good influence, Rob."

"I'm trying to resurrect the old Jeff Chartrand, but it seems I'm only partially succeeding."

"Sixteen years is a long time, Rob. It changes a man, and I don't know if I want to become that man again. He was not a pleasant individual."

"Events may not give you a choice. This thing is far from over. You want to punish the people responsible for your brother's murder, don't you? They didn't only murder him but also your sister-in-law and your nephew. Don't forget that." Rob paused but kept his eyes on the traffic. "These people pretend to be law abiding citizens. They have lawyers and judges in their pockets. They have money. You know how our legal system works. They will never do time. You may have to take the law into your own hands, my friend, if you want revenge."

"Won't that bring me down to their level? I won't be any better than them," Jeff said, a bitter taste in his mouth.

"To fight them you have to get down to their level or you'll lose. You'll have to be ruthless and be able to kill them in cold blood. Only then will you get justice." Rob spoke with a hard voice, cold and emotionless. It sent a shiver down Jeff's spine. He knew Rob spoke the truth and that made him angry.

It had taken him years to forget the things he did when he was part of Grey Ops. He had done them without asking questions, without compunction. Only years later his conscience had begun to awaken feelings of guilt and remorse.

"You are a cop, Jeff. You had to harden yourself to do your job efficiently. You shot Galliano and his right hand man," Rob said.

"That was self-defense. They would have killed me had I not shot first."

"So will these people. Once you are on their list, there is no escaping. You have to make that first shot."

"We'll see," Jeff said, watching the car in the mirror. He had no doubt now they were being followed and wished he had a gun. He felt naked without it. "I think I'll need a gun," he said to Rob.

Rob smiled. "Now you're talking. I brought a couple of guns in our luggage. As soon as we get to our hotel, you can have yours."

When they arrived at the Holiday Inn, the Cadillac passed them and disappeared into the traffic.

Jeff breathed a sigh of relief. "I think they just wanted to check us out and make sure we told Mariano the truth about where we are staying," he said.

"Looks that way, but I'm not relaxing." Rob drove the car into the parking lot.

Before they went for supper, Rob searched through his luggage and took out a gun. A Beretta. "I didn't bring a holster," he apologized. "You'll have to stick it into your belt."

"Good enough," Jeff growled. "I feel better already." He smiled. "Sometimes I think you are an old man hiding in a young body. You remind me a lot of my tenth grade teacher."

Rob shrugged. "Maybe I was a teacher in one of my former lives. Who knows?"

"It is more likely you were a Viking or a warrior in Japan or China. If you were a teacher you taught the art of war."

"You believe in reincarnation?"

"Not really, but I won't dispute it may be possible. I've wondered a lot about those child prodigies, the ones who play instruments and compose music at an early age. That kind of stuff makes you think and almost believe in reincarnation. I was raised in the catholic faith, and the church certainly denies it. It doesn't fit into the system of belief."

Rob snorted. "Of course not. Therefore, it is rejected. That's why I'm an agnostic. Sort of. I believe in the materialistic world. As far as I'm concerned, there is no god. How else do you explain the state of the world we live in? God is a figment of the imagination."

"I do believe in some kind of Supreme Being, but like most people, I don't really know what exactly I believe. Certainly not the things I've been taught, not any more." Jeff sighed. "I think cynical people like you are lucky in a way because you believe in nothing. You don't battle with yourself, feeling guilty about your faith. You know where you stand. True believers, if there are actually any, are also lucky. They have something to lean on when they are lost and frustrated. They never feel alone."

"And you?" Rob asked.

"It depends. Sometimes I am happy with what I believe. At other times, I get frustrated and I am full of doubt. I ask about the reason for the bad things that happen to good people and the good things bad people seem to enjoy. I try to make sense out of it."

"Whom do you ask?"

Jeff laughed softly. "Whom indeed? I ask God, whoever he is, wherever he hides these days."

"Ever get any answers?" Rob smiled, but he seemed serious.

"What do you think?" Jeff took the gun and stuck it into his belt behind his back. "I hope I don't have to use it. Not tonight anyway."

* * * *

"I believe we should pay our friend Jimmy Marco a visit. I'd like to take another look at that building." Jeff finished his second cup of coffee. It helped to calm his nerves.

They walked into the office of Nova Investments shortly after ten.

Mindy sat behind her desk doing her nails. It seemed she didn't have anything else to do. She gave them a bright smile when they stepped out of the elevator into the plush foyer. "You've come back," she said.

"Yes, we'd like to have another word with Mr. Marco," Jeff said.

"Oh, I'm sorry. Jimmy isn't with our firm anymore." She sounded genuinely sorry.

"What happened?" Rob asked.

She shrugged her pretty shoulders and shook her long hair out of her face. Looking around, she said in a whisper, "Mr. Hardini fired him. If you ask me, they had a fight over something. It happened right after you two gentlemen talked to Mr. Hardini."

"That is too bad. Is Mr. Hardini in?"

"No, he is out meeting with a client. He won't be back until tomorrow." She inspected her nails. "I'm all be myself in the office right now. Everyone is gone. Jimmy used to be the only one usually hanging around the office. He was a lot of fun. I miss him."

"He seemed like a nice guy," Rob agreed. He gave her a disengaging smile. "A beautiful girl like you should never be alone."

She let out a short giggle. "Are you flirting with me?"

"How can I resist the urge?" Rob chuckled. "Would it be possible to have a look in Mr. Hardini's office? We were supposed to pick up some papers." He smiled. "Actually, not until tomorrow, but we were close by and hoped to find Mr. Hardini in his office."

"You want me to let you into his office?"

"If it's possible. We wouldn't want you to get in trouble over it. But then again, you might just get some points with Mr. Hardini for taking the initiative. You see, we were working on an important deal and time is of the essence." He rubbed his chin. "It's too bad, we might just loose out now. As will your company. If you let us get the material we need it might even earn you a promotion, Mindy."

Mindy looked doubtful. "I don't know."

"It's up to you, sweetheart, but this is a tremendous opportunity. You know what they say about being at the right place at the right time. Opportunities only come to those who are prepared. This is one of those times."

"He'll find out."

"Of course he'll find out. You'll want him to know that you were the one who made it possible. That you've displayed some initiative. Come on, what do you say?"

Her eyes moved from Rob to Jeff. "I don't know," she said again. "You look like a couple of nice gentlemen. You wouldn't do anything stupid now, would you?"

Rob raised both hands. "Scout's honor. I promise."

"All right."

"Good girl." Rob reached across the desk and patted her hand. "You won't regret it. Oh, one more thing, before we forget. Do you have Jimmy's address handy?"

"Sure. Do you want it?"

"Yes, please."

She checked her computer and then she wrote something onto a piece of paper. Handing it to Rob, she said, "If you see him, tell him to give me a call, okay?"

Rob nodded. "No problem."

They followed her to Hardini's office. Jeff couldn't believe how things seemed to turn out in their favor. It didn't really comfort him. Something eventually had to go wrong.

Mindy hesitated by the door, obviously not sure if she should stay or get back to her desk. Jeff took the decision from her. "Maybe you should go and watch the elevator in case a client shows up." He laughed softly. "You wouldn't want anyone coming in and robbing the place."

"Oh my god, no. My purse is on my desk." She rushed away, leaving them alone.

Rob grinned at Jeff. "This is better than I expected. Maybe we'll get lucky for a change."

"I'll look in the filing cabinet while you check out the computer," Jeff said. He walked over to the large cabinet on one wall and pulled out the first drawer. Rifling through the files as quickly as possible, he didn't find anything suspicious until he opened the fifth drawer. Right in the back, he saw a thick file labeled *Mariano*.

When he took it out and opened it, he let out a low whistle. "I think I just found the mother lode," he said.

"So did I," Rob said. "I don't know if this guy is stupid or feels so secure he doesn't think he needs to hide things. None of the files have passwords. None are encrypted."

Jeff walked over to Rob and looked at one of the opened files. "I think this is the same information I found. Want to have a look?"

Rob shuffled through the stuff Jeff handed him and nodded. "The same. I guess Mr. Hardini doesn't trust computers. Why else would he print it all out and keep files the old-fashioned way?"

"Computers crash. Maybe he isn't that stupid."

"He could save it on a disk or flash drive." Rob shook his head. "I guess I'd better get busy. Put your stuff back, Jeff. We don't want him to get suspicious." He pulled a flash drive out of his pocket and connected it to the port in front of the console. Then he began downloading the files.

They left the office fifteen minutes later.

"Did you find what you were looking for?" Mindy asked.

"Oh, yes, we certainly did." He bent across the desk. "Do us a favor. Don't tell Mr. Hardini about our visit. We want it to be a surprise when the deal is done. Okay?"

"Okay." She giggled. "I'm looking forward to that surprise. This is so exciting."

"It sure is."

When they took the elevator down to the main floor, Jeff shook his head. "I didn't know girls like her actually existed. Could she really be that ignorant?"

"Admittedly, she is not the smartest girl I've ever met," Rob said, "but she did have a nice ass. I'm sure she has some qualifications that lift her above the rest."

"I hope so."

"We should go and pay Marco a visit. Now that he's been fired, maybe he'll be more amiable to provide us with information he held back. He certainly doesn't owe Hardini anything."

"Agreed," Jeff said. "I feel guilty for being the cause of Jimmy Marco's dismissal. I almost liked the kid."

When they arrived at the address Mindy gave them, they saw a couple of police cars and an ambulance parked in front of the apartment building Marco lived in. They parked their car and walked the short distance, wondering what that was all about.

One of the cops stopped them when they approached the entrance to the building. "Nobody is allowed to enter," he told them. "This is a crime scene."

"What happened?"

The cop seemed eager to talk to someone. "Ah, the usual. Some guy got shot last night. It happens in this neighborhood all the time."

"Do you have any details on the shooting?" Jeff asked.

The cop gave him a quizzical look. "Are you a reporter?"

"No, we are investigating an insurance fraud. The man we want to talk to lives in this building."

"Insurance fraud?" A bystander chuckled beside them. "It wouldn't surprise me. He's been in some kind of trouble as long as I knew him. He used to run with one of the gangs, you know?"

A sudden feeling of foreboding made Jeff ask, "What's they guy's name?"

"Jimmy Marco."

"Jimmy Marco?" Jeff repeated, shocked by the revelation. "He's the man we came to see. He works for Nova Investments."

"Used to," the bystander said, blowing air through his nostril. "He got fired yesterday. Again, no surprise here. Having a guy like Jimmy working for an insurance company is like putting a fox into a henhouse. I knew he wouldn't last long."

"We never said he committed a crime," Jeff said, feeling irritated by the man's comments. "We just came to ask him some questions." He shrugged. "I guess that's not possible now."

The cop had moved away and Jeff felt relieved. The last thing they needed right now was to draw attention to their presence here.

"Let's go," he said to Rob.

Walking briskly beside Jeff, Rob said, "I'm not saying we should feel guilty, but inadvertently we caused Jimmy Marco's death. It is obvious we've stepped on some toes. I have a feeling this isn't over. You have your gun?"

Jeff became suddenly aware of the slight pressure in his back. In a way, it was reassuring. "I do but I hope we don't have to use it. We can't afford to advertise our involvement with Mariano. I have no doubt he is behind this. Hardini must have reported our visit to him. By now Mariano knows we are not who we said we were."

"Let's get back to our hotel," Rob said. "I'd like to find a computer and have a look at the flash drive. There has to be a library nearby."

They were close to downtown, when Jeff noticed a black car coming up behind them.

A Cadillac.

It began to pass them. Jeff had been watching and, looking past the driver at the passenger, he saw the gun aimed at him through the Cadillac's open window.

"Gun!" he cursed loudly, clawing at his own weapon.

He ducked, heard the crack of a gunshot, pitched forward as Rob slammed his foot on the brakes. Then he had his own gun out and, leaning out of his window, he fired at the Cadillac, which had pulled slightly ahead.

He aimed at the driver.

The Cadillac swerved suddenly, moved in front of their car, and then it crashed into a signpost.

Rob slammed again on his brakes and managed to stop the car before it hit the Cadillac. Jeff jumped out, gun in hand. When he reached the other car, he saw the passenger slumped in his seat. Blood trickled from a gash in his forehead. He was either dead or just unconscious. His sunglasses had slipped off his face and lay on the dashboard. Jeff heard Rob opening the door on the driver's side and saw him pulling the driver out of the vehicle.

He put his hand against the neck of the man still in the car and detected a pulse, wondering fleetingly why the airbags of the Cadillac had not been activated by the crash.

"This guy's dead," Rob said from the other side. "You got him right in the head."

Jeff decided to leave the man in his seat. He checked the inside pocket of the man's suit and pulled out his wallet, pocketed it. "Take his ID," he told Rob. "Then let's get out of here."

Most cars on the road had driven by, throwing only curious glances at the scene. He saw one car stopping behind theirs and a man getting out.

"Do you have a cell?" Jeff asked him.

The man nodded. "Call the cops. Tell them we'll be checking in with the report later. We're pursuing another suspect."

The man nodded again. "Sure, detective. No problem."

Jeff joined Rob in their car and then they took off.

"Damn it!" Jeff swore. "That's all we needed."

"It was bound to happen," Rob said.

"Fuck it anyway. I hope that guy didn't get a good look at us or we'll have the cops looking for us."

"The dead guy," Rob said. "He looked a lot like Hardini."

"Oh, man, don't tell me." Jeff took the wallet Rob handed him and opened it. "Son of a bitch!" he cursed. "The guy's name was Terrence Hardini."

"Benny's brother. I'm not surprised." Rob shrugged. "Looks like the Godfather marked us for death."

"Now I'm really pissed off," Jeff said. "He's had my brother killed. Now he's after us. I wonder how he ties into all of this. I can't imagine that he is the one behind this whole deal. There are more people involved and we'd better find out who."

Rob parked the car, hoping the guy with the cell phone didn't remember the model. They went back into their hotel room.

"Let's go for lunch," Rob said. "I'm starved."

"I'm not very hungry." Jeff put his gun on the table and looked at it. "We'll have to ditch this. I don't feel like spending time in a cell in Chicago."

"Wait until we've talked to Mariano. You might still need it," Rob suggested.

"Do you think it's wise to go back there?" Jeff doubted the wisdom of going back into Mariano's stronghold.

"He needs to be dealt with, Jeff. You know that as well as I. If we don't take him out, we'll be paying for it later. He doesn't know yet who we are, but he will find out. Sooner or later, someone will recognize you even with your disguise. That man had your brother and his family killed. Murdered in cold blood. We can't let him get away with that."

Jeff knew Rob was right. Mariano had too many connections. He would never pay for his crimes. This one and the ones he committed in the past. Even if he wasn't the puller of strings, he was one of them. He was one of the main players. Eliminating him would not stop the sale of weapons or change the way the world was running, but there would be one less criminal walking the Earth.

"When do you want to do it?" he asked.

"Today," Rob said. "Right after lunch."

End of Book Two
To be continued in Book Three
Tarnished Valor